# *DO NOT DISTURB*

An Erotica Collection

This novel is entirely a work of fiction.
The names, characters and incidents portrayed in it are
the work of the author's imagination. Any resemblance to
actual persons, living or dead, events or localities is
entirely coincidental.

*Mischief*
An imprint of HarperCollins*Publishers*
77–85 Fulham Palace Road,
Hammersmith, London W6 8JB

www.mischiefbooks.com

A Paperback Original 2013

First published in Great Britain in ebook format by
HarperCollins*Publishers* 2012

Copyright
*Something Extra* © Flora Dain
*Room 414* © Jason Rubis
*Ice Is Nice* © Louise Hooker
*Flashing* © Rachel Kramer Bussel
*Suite Surrender* © Willow Sears
*A Touch of Class, a Bit of Rough* © Rose de Fer
*An Airport, Anywhere* © Elizabeth Coldwell
*Poisons* © Cèsar Sanchez Zapata
*Scheduling Conferences* © Kathleen Tudor
*Ssshh, No Speaking!* © Tabitha Kitten

The author asserts the moral right to
be identified as the author of this work

A catalogue record for this book is
available from the British Library

ISBN-13: 9780007553433

Find out more about HarperCollins and the environment at
**www.harpercollins.co.uk/green**

All rights reserved. No part of this publication may be
reproduced, stored in a retrieval system, or transmitted,
in any form or by any means, electronic, mechanical,
photocopying, recording or otherwise, without the prior
permission of the publishers.

## Contents

| | |
|---|---:|
| Something Extra<br>*Flora Dain* | 1 |
| Room 414<br>*Jason Rubis* | 19 |
| Ice Is Nice<br>*Louise Hooker* | 39 |
| Flashing<br>*Rachel Kramer Bussel* | 62 |
| Suite Surrender<br>*Willow Sears* | 81 |
| A Touch of Class, a Bit of Rough<br>*Rose de Fer* | 107 |
| An Airport, Anywhere<br>*Elizabeth Coldwell* | 125 |
| Poisons<br>*Cèsar Sanchez Zapata* | 141 |
| Scheduling Conferences<br>*Kathleen Tudor* | 156 |
| Ssshh No Speaking!<br>*Tabitha Kitten* | 172 |

## *Something Extra*
## *Flora Dain*

'Open your legs. Wider. Now push out that delectable little ass. I want you spread and ready.'

The voice in my earphone is deep and stirring. Whenever I hear it I melt, like I'm chocolate cake.

Maybe to him I *am* chocolate cake – with cream on.

It's late evening and I'm leaning on the bar of a plush hotel. The barman gives me a long look as he shakes my cocktail.

I guess he's used to seeing women dressed like this. I'm heavily made up, with piled-up hair, a skimpy, revealing satin dress and high heels.

I'm even wearing diamonds – real ones.

I may look expensive but I feel cheap. Or maybe it's the other way round. Tonight I'm so excited I can't think straight.

I can also feel colour in my cheeks and a sparkle in

my eye. It's not just from excitement. There's more than a touch of fear in there somewhere too.

I don't do this very often.

'Lean forward. Keep your legs straight. I want the men around you to wonder if you're wearing panties. Move a little.'

I sway provocatively as I sip my drink. I'm hot now, partly from shame, partly from sheer, thumping *arousal*.

He knows perfectly well I'm not wearing any. I was ordered to leave them off.

His low command sends a shaft of heat straight to my groin.

Has he any idea how short this dress is? If I lean forward any further everyone here will know for sure …

The men around me all know I'm here. No one's looking at me but I'm a female on heat. I can sense their interest. They're waiting to see who's with me.

'Are you OK, Miss?'

Even the barman's curious now. There are other people waiting to be served but he ignores them. Maybe he thinks I've had too much to drink.

The earpieces are wired to my phone. To everyone else around here it must look like I'm listening to music. I smile at him and nod.

He colours a little and looks pleased.

Is he going to chat me up? This might be a complication. But the men are tired of waiting and soon get his attention.

'Now take a step back and arch your neck. Make sure all the men at the bar can get a good look at your tits.' That voice, *his* voice, purrs again in my ear and I take a careful step back, hoping I don't stab anyone's foot. These heels are lethal.

Several of the men are openly staring now, eyeing me as if I'm not only chocolate cake but the last piece left on the plate.

This could get tricky.

I know what they're thinking but so might the management. Any minute now someone might decide to throw me out.

I feel warmth behind me, a brush of fabric. Heat flares deep in my belly.

*He's here.*

He leans forward and places his hands on the bar at either side of me in a frank, alpha-territorial land-grab. From somewhere above and behind me he calls to the barman, who scuttles over.

No waiting around for Mr Alpha. He always gets instant service.

'Another cocktail for the lady. For me a scotch. Make it a double.'

The barman looks a little scared. 'Yes, Sir. On the tab?'

I feel my earpieces being gently removed. Mr Alpha leans close to my ear as he unlaces the wiring and reaches round to retrieve my phone from somewhere deep between my breasts.

His fingers deliberately graze my nipple. It stiffens and prods against the thin satin, telling anyone who happens to be watching that I'm a needy, greedy slut. I can almost hear him think it as he slips my technology into his pocket.

'Now walk slowly over to the table by the palm and wait.'

I do as I'm told. Men's eyes follow me all the way. There's some sort of corporate event taking place tonight and I'm one of the only women around.

I'm certainly the only woman dressed like this.

The table is a small circle perched on a stand. People are discouraged from sitting for long. They're urged to stand while they drink so they can join the dance floor.

He follows me and sets down our drinks on the little circle between us. We stand side by side, our backs to the palm. He lifts his scotch and toasts me in a mild, sardonic greeting. I raise my second cocktail of the evening and touch his glass.

Our eyes lock, his full of fire, mine, I'm sure, bright with excitement.

Slowly he inspects my full, painted lips, my bare throat and my deep cleavage. As his eyes roam over me his gaze falls on my upper breasts, pink with my embarrassment, rosy with arousal.

He looks amused. *He's enjoying this.*

I know what he likes. And he knows I find his demands hard to meet.

That's why he makes them.

'You're late.'

I feel a tremor go through me. This could mean trouble.

I smile confidently, my fingers idly running up and down the stem of my cocktail glass in a casual imitation of a lewd caress. Slowly I spear the little cherry and suck it with pursed, baby-doll lips.

His hand steals up the back of my thigh and encounters my naked self, shamefully exposed under my short, frilly hem and already disgracefully, lustfully wet.

His fingertips explore a little, while his steady gaze dares me to keep still. He asks me about my journey and how my day has gone. I do my best to keep calm enough to answer while all the time I tingle and seethe, desperately wanting to giggle and wriggle and *shout*.

His fingers slide in deeper and my voice falters. He frowns while I struggle to regain control. It's unwise to provoke him this early in the evening. It might lead to – complications.

His eyes narrow. 'Any particular reason? Or did you just think I like to be kept waiting?'

I plop the cherry back in my drink, hoping to distract him. I slide the tip of my tongue slowly along my lower lip. The toe of my shoe moves gently along the inner edge of his trouser leg, just above the ankle.

## Do Not Disturb

His fingers take instant advantage of my splayed leg and his hand is now fully engaged with my nether regions, sending flames shooting all over my skin. A trickle of moisture runs down the inside of my thigh.

My faltering apology reaches the ears of the kindly barman, who is now collecting glasses from the next stand. He glances over at me with real concern and then looks away quickly as Mr Alpha catches his eye.

The barman has kind eyes and tousled blond hair with streaks in it. He's good-looking in a windswept, boyish kind of way. Mr Alpha continues to watch him as he moves around the tables.

'Do you know each other?' I joke.

'We might have played the odd game of squash,' he says airily.

*Oh? When?*

'He's very athletic.' He turns to me, his expression opaque. 'Why? Do you like him?'

I colour and lower my eyelashes, unsure where this is going. 'He seems nice.'

He *knows* him? What else has he kept from me?

'Will he be joining us later?' My whisper is barely audible but I see his lips twitch at the corner. Clearly this has also occurred to him.

'Possibly. I'll think about it. Dance?'

We join the other couples swaying on the dance floor but now I'm nervous.

The lights are low and the coloured spots play over the crowd, breaking up sight lines, confusing the view, but he always dances close. And when he dances close he holds me firmly at the back, his hand now low on my waist, then lower.

His fingers move gently, their warmth sending shivers through me.

I feel his thumb through the thin fabric, pressing into my muscles, teasing me. His grip hoists my brief hem a touch higher all the time we move and I begin quietly to panic.

Will someone see? Will they notice that underneath I'm bare and exposed, and shamefully, outrageously *wet* ...?

He dances beautifully. He is tall and powerful looking, with regular, classical features that make most women melt, most men jealous. In a crowded room most eyes are on him most of the time, so when we dance they're on me as well.

I know I'm lucky but he's very demanding.

He works hard and makes a lot of money. In these situations I'm expected to look my best. That takes time and effort.

Like Dolly Parton says, it costs an awful lot to look this cheap.

And the effects can be unpredictable. That's one reason I'm nervous.

The other is the way he's looking at me now.

*Do Not Disturb*

'Shall we go up? You first. I'll follow in a few minutes.'

As I leave I see from the corner of my eye that he's talking to the barman. They look easy together, like they know each other well.

I strain to catch what they're saying. '… Something extra for the weekend …'

I lose the rest in a sudden swell of music.

They share a smile at this old-fashioned male saying.

I turn away with a frown. He's got no *condoms*? How odd.

No matter. I've got plenty.

\* \* \*

Our suite is huge, with views all over the city. We leave the drapes open on purpose, partly to maximise the thrill of what comes next, partly so we can see it. The windows are glossy with night sky and make perfect mirrors.

The door opens and softly closes and I know he's here. He comes up behind me, his reflection looming over my shoulder like a demon in a painting. He winds his arms around me and fastens his mouth on the side of my neck.

'At last. I thought we'd never get here.'

I swivel in his arms and he fastens his lips on mine, plundering my mouth like he's starved. His hands are all over me, feeling, probing, turning the thin silk dress into a limp dishrag, making me feel the same way.

'Shall I take it off?' I murmur playfully when he finally releases my mouth.

His eyes burn into mine and I see a flash of anger. *Whoa.* Now what?

'No. Leave it on. You've got some explaining to do.'

He takes firm hold of my wrist and drags me over to the bed. He sits down with an angry flop and pushes me down onto my knees.

As he does so he's tearing at his clothes and soon they are flung at random all over the floor and he is sitting naked before me, his manhood, huge and erect, jutting aggressively into my face.

*This is so hot ...* I could look at him like this for hours.

'There's the small matter of you being late. Two minutes. Explain.' His jaw is rigid, his eyes blazing.

He is very aroused.

Automatically I put my hands behind my back and clasp them loosely together. We used to do this often, but it's been a while ...

'Forgive me, Sir,' I manage. 'I'd no idea. I thought I was on time.'

It's a feeble excuse at best and nowhere near enough to let me off the hook he's planning.

'Two minutes. How many seconds in a minute?'

'Sixty, sir.' My whisper is a little shaky. I know what is coming.

'And in two?'

## Do Not Disturb

'A hundred and twenty, Sir.' I hang my head.

His eyes narrow with a terrifying gleam. 'Then you'll get a spanking of one hundred and twenty strokes. Sixty now. Get over my knee.'

With a surge of excitement I clamber into position and he pulls up my scanty, rumpled skirt.

First he teases me with lube, his fingers lingering provocatively at my openings and then easing deep into one of them. *That one.* I gasp. After a second he probes it with something tapered and frighteningly solid. That feels lubed too.

'Had you forgotten? I promised you something new. Relax, it's going in whether you like it or not'

It's a butt plug. I clench my teeth as he slides the huge, obscene thing into place. My muscles grip it eagerly. My clit gives an answering jolt of arousal – and then it begins.

He starts light but the blows come thick and fast. In all the excitement my breasts tumble out of my plunging neckline and bounce against his thigh.

Every few strokes he pauses to massage and caress me. His touch is unbearably gentle. Tears smart at the back of my eyes from the sting of the blows but they spill over at the tenderness of his touch. Then he starts again.

After a while I come violently, crying out for a pause to catch my breath and savour the pleasure, but he carries on, ignoring my pleas.

During the next ten strokes my excitement begins

to build again and this time I can feel his erection jut painfully into my leg. I'm poised on the brink of another massive orgasm when he shifts position and cruelly moves his knee away from my aching, burning centre.

Now the jolt of his hand prods me ever closer to climax but I never quite reach it. My tears and whimpers get louder as I try to wriggle back into position.

Deliberately he fends me off and forces me to keep still. I can hear a low growl of arousal deep in his throat. 'You want to come again? When I say so, not before.'

*Ow.* Harsh words, but just. I feel hotter than ever.

At last the spanking is done and I lie on the bed panting with my burning backside high in the air. His hands are hot now. With one last, glorious fondle he massages me again and then pushes me back onto my knees.

'Now a small token of thanks. Take it in your mouth.'

He's still angry. Most of his rage seems to be centred in his purplish, swollen erection. It almost burns in my mouth. As I swirl my tongue around the silky skin he shudders convulsively and lets out a deep male groan.

'Hey, easy. We've a long way to go yet.'

Easy is impossible, his cock is too big. It's all I can do to swallow but he pulls me forward a few times to set up a rhythm and soon I'm gulping lustily, catching my breath between strokes and stifling my gag reflex as best I can.

I *love* this, choking on him, being filled by him. I could do this for hours ...

*Do Not Disturb*

He pulls me over his knee again.

At that moment there's a knock at the door. It opens softly and *someone comes in.*

'Room service, Sir.'

It's the kindly barman. He holds a tray aloft, bearing another cocktail and two scotches. He pauses just inside the door, transfixed, his eyes locked on my burning rear end, my spilling breasts and the huge, jutting erection clearly visible below my arched body.

'Where would you like it, Sir?'

Mr Alpha pushes me off his knee and gives me a stern look as he commands me to keep still. I kneel obediently, glad of a chance to catch my breath. He strides purposefully over to the barman, commanding me to stand.

As I do so the barman stares at me, taking me in. He pales.

I flush crimson and dash away a tear.

Mr Alpha towers over him, magnificent, erect, *rampant*. He looks sensational. The barman is visibly moved, but his glance keeps stealing towards me.

He lowers his voice. 'Are you sure about this, Sir? She's gorgeous. I could come back later –'

Mr Alpha's jaw stiffens and the poor man falters into silence. They continue to eye each other.

I'm worried now. Is it me who's intruding here?

'Chill. It's just a bit of fun. Have a drink.' Mr Alpha

gently takes the tray out of his hand, sets it down on a side table and hands him a scotch.

It's then that I realise – he's brought *three* drinks.

He's here by invitation.

At that moment Mr Alpha glances across and my fears are laid to rest. Mr Alpha's physique clearly overawes the barman but when Mr Alpha eyes him something in his look remains veiled.

When he looks at me – *pow*. There's the heat.

Now he fingers the barman's lapel, a seemingly intimate gesture that only seconds before I might have misread.

'You're a little overdressed.'

The barman begins to tear at his buttons but Mr Alpha places a hand on his arm. He signals to me to come forward. 'She'll do it.'

I step close to the little barman and smile shyly up into his face. 'Are you sure you're up for this?'

He looks at me wildly. 'You *think*? Lady, this is all my birthdays rolled into one.'

And I notice that he too is erect. So slowly, carefully, I take off his clothes. He sighs and closes his eyes long before I've finished.

I feel a little shaky under Mr Alpha's stern gaze, but he looks on in silence. When the barman is naked I move my hands slowly over his soft, fair body.

He's shorter than Mr Alpha and less well endowed.

## Do Not Disturb

All the same his erection's pretty impressive and very responsive. As my fingers stray into the soft, golden curls nestling around his root he shudders, lips parted, showing pretty white teeth.

His cock leaps and twitches at my unfamiliar touch.

'Easy. If he comes too soon you'll spoil the fun.' Mr Alpha's deep growl rumbles between us and makes us both jump. Guiltily I snatch my hand away.

The barman opens wide, lustful eyes and takes a long, shaky breath. 'Wow.'

I smile. A film of sweat on his forehead is matting some of the blond streaks into little damp curls. He looks like some hungry, grown-up cherub – good enough to eat.

Mr Alpha eyes us both with interest. 'Ready?'

'You bet.' The barman is eyeing me like I'm his next meal and he hasn't eaten for a while.

Mr Alpha's eyes narrow. 'Aren't we forgetting something?'

The barman looks instantly terrified. 'What?'

Mr Alpha holds up two foil packets. 'These.'

The barman automatically reaches for one but Mr Alpha holds them higher, out of his reach. 'Uh-uh. She'll put them on.'

He gets behind me and puts his hands on my shoulders, forcing me to my knees.

This is beyond exciting. I can scarcely breathe. The orgasm I was denied earlier is pounding against my sex now, demanding release. If something doesn't happen soon I'll explode.

I reach up for the packet but Mr Alpha captures my wrists and pulls my arms firmly behind me. 'Not so fast. Show our guest some respect. You'll put it on with your mouth. Lick him first.'

The barman's cock bucks as I lean forward. He smells nice – very clean, like he's just washed. I lick nervously at the broad silky head. Mr Alpha's own erection juts imperiously into my neck. His grip on my arms is like iron, and I can feel the heat from his powerful thighs at either side of me.

I know what he wants me to do – wet the barman's erection all over so the condom will be just that little bit more sensitive once it's in place, but I've never done it *like this* or to another man.

Wickedness takes on a whole new dimension.

At last his tool is thoroughly wet and by some miracle of self-control the barman has managed not to come. Now for the condom. Mr Alpha places it in my mouth and I ease it on with my lips and my tongue, nipping and tugging at the end to fix it in place while the barman groans.

'Now me.' Mr Alpha releases my arms and the barman steps behind to take his place. Mr Alpha towers before me and his erection is so big now I wonder if I shall manage this, but his wonderful taste and the feel of his ridged skin propel me to new heights of skill. At last I lean back, pleased with myself.

He has watched me throughout, a deep, burning gleam in his eyes his only reaction to what I know must be a pretty intense experience.

The two men loom over me, looking deep into each other's eyes. They seem to communicate on a different level now.

At Mr Alpha's slight nod the barman hoists me under the arms and holds me up, my toes just touching the floor. He's stronger than he looks. He holds me suspended in mid-air while Mr Alpha slowly removes the butt plug.

As it slides out I give a deep sigh and nearly come again. A stern look from Mr Alpha prevents me. I'd almost forgotten it was there and now I feel empty, open, abandoned.

At that moment he gives the barman another nod and I feel the head of the barman's sheathed erection prod gently at my opening, filling the gap, and then without warning he surges up inside me.

I cry out, startled at the suddenness of it, and then Mr Alpha takes a step forward, his eyes burning into mine, and he enters me from the front.

*Oh, yes ...*

They ease in fully and wait a second, eyeing each other over my shoulder like gymnasts poised for some intricate move, and then they start to thrust ...

It's glorious. I've never in all my life felt so filled, so used, so *hot*. I come in minutes, the spasms rocketing through me, tipping the barman over the edge, and he comes with a shriek.

Mr Alpha is taking his time. He can stave off pleasure for hours. Now he's smiling and slowly withdraws, easing me onto my knees. He slaps the barman on the back. 'Thanks. You were terrific. I'll take over now. We'll settle up later.'

The barman dresses quickly and leaves, giving me a fond little half wave as he closes the door.

\* \* \*

Now we are alone. Mr Alpha circles around me, his gaze stern. 'Did you enjoy that?'

I eye him playfully. 'Did *you*?'

His eyes darken. 'Mind your manners. Lean over the bed.'

I double up over the edge of the bed, my legs splayed wide, my head on the mattress and my ass high in the air. I'm all glowing now and he spanks me again, really hard this time. It's wildly arousing. At last I feel his hands smoothing over my punished, burning cheeks with long, loving sweeps, easing his fingers into my passages, driving me to distraction.

'You're so beautiful. I've never seen anything so infuriating as you touching that blond. If I ever see you do that again I'll –'

*Do Not Disturb*

He breaks off as he plunges into me from behind, his erection now so big and so hot I feel I've been invaded by a volcano. He pounds into me time and again, his thrusts long, hot and savage.

'You'll what?' I grin between gasps.

I almost feel his wave of fury as his climax begins to swell his cock even bigger. 'I'll fuck you rigid, like this.'

With a great shout he comes inside me. We collapse together on the bed, laughing, ecstatic and spent.

\* \* \*

Tomorrow we'll be on our way home and all this will be just a memory. While he drives I'll gaze adoringly at his profile. From time to time he'll touch my hand or stroke my thigh.

We lead busy, happy lives, full of family, full of love. We get rarely get the chance to be completely on our own. Sometimes we like to play wicked, grown-up games.

I work hard too. He knows me well. And he knows that once in a while, to keep things spicy, I need something just that little bit *extra*.

# Room 414
## Jason Rubis

'Lazy ...'

Reflecting on it later, it would occur to Ryan how natural waking up next to her had seemed – so natural he didn't wonder at her presence for even a moment. Of course, the whole scene was awash in sleepy pleasures; the bed was warm, her body as perfumed and sweetly soft as the early-morning haze clouding his mind. She lay with an arm draped across his chest, long legs holding one of his scissored between. Holding him tight, and stroking him with a somehow proprietary air. As though she intended to never release him. Normally Ryan tended to squirm when a lover held him too tightly during the night, but he felt he could spend a happy eternity dozing in this one's arms.

'Tell me ... what am I to do with such a lazy man?' Her mouth was as soft as her hands, whispering the

*Do Not Disturb*

words into his ear. An accent – British? There had been a woman in his office who spoke like that, a transfer from the London office. Wonderful, sexy accent. Those round vowels. Like listening to music when she spoke.

What was the woman's name – Pamela? What was sexy Pam doing in a New York hotel room with him?

Ryan strained upward against the mystery woman's limbs. Laughter sounded lightly in his ear, and the limbs tightened against him, holding him down. He made no attempt to escape.

'No, no ... *mine*.' She licked his ear, laughing again, but lower this time, a little growl/purr deep in her throat. The scent of bed-warmed skin seemed to briefly intensify.

*She's excited. She wants me.* The thought didn't just stiffen his cock; he found it flattering, as if she were a celebrity or some person of note. He reached for her arms and she moved to straddle his waist, smiled down at him.

She wasn't Pam.

'Where you going, hey? Got a date?'

She had coffee-and-cream skin and tousled black hair, squiggly locks of it hanging in wide dark eyes. A broad, strong nose that was almost too strong for her delicate face; it *would* have been too strong if it weren't for those eyes and the smiling red mouth. Her breasts were small, little creamy handfuls with dark, hard nipples.

'Who's the lucky girl, then? Anyone I know?'

She pressed down on his chest with both palms,

grinning as she shifted her hips. A firm, wet weight grinding atop his now fully erect cock.

'Told you ... *this* is mine. I don't share my toys. Those other girls can go find their own.'

What had he done the previous night? He had gone out, met her at some bar?

'And you know ... I feel like playing with it a bit more.' She rose briefly on her knees, groped for something hidden by a fold in the bedclothes. At first he thought it was a chocolate; a moment later, when she held it up for his inspection, he laughed at himself; it was a condom. She had it unwrapped in a moment, then she slid both hands between her legs. Ryan felt her fingers groping for his hardness, rolling the condom on.

He lay back, unresisting. Yeah, he must have gone out last night. It was the only explanation. Because here was the proof, horny and smiling, getting ready to fuck him. He had met this woman and brought her back to his room ...

Except that he hadn't.

Once he had that thought his mind began clearing, his thoughts beginning to process at something like normal speed. Glancing to one side, he saw his laptop still open on the table by the window, a stack of binders beside it, dishes from room service beside those.

No, he hadn't gone out. He remembered now. He had stayed in and worked. Because Wilson wanted the numbers by next morning. And next morning – *this* morning – he had to be at La Guardia at nine to catch his plane and he didn't want to work on the flight home. He had worked until two and gone to bed alone.

He didn't know this woman. He had no idea at all who she was.

Inexplicably, the thought did nothing to calm his erection. It enflamed him, brought on a surge of excitement so powerful he thought he could almost taste it, like a bite of lemon. Before he knew it, he was sliding into her, and it was good, the sensation so beautiful he found himself immediately surrendering to it. She was tight, and so wet he thought he could hear himself moving in her. Ryan grabbed handfuls of the sheets at his waist, resisting the urge to reach up and touch her face, focusing only on the need to push up into her again and again.

'Ooohh ... yeah, lover. Yeah, my *baby*.'

She was riding him, leaning forward to grip the edges of the headboard, hips grinding, encouraging him to thrust hard and harder.

*Who is she? Who the fuck is this woman, where'd she come from?* The question was like a whining voice in his ear. Five years ago he wouldn't have even heard it. Five years ago he would have been thanking God and all the stars for dropping her into his bed like this. But he was thirty now. There were considerations.

Still. Considerations didn't soften him and they sure

as hell didn't make him want to pull out. She grinned down at him, ran a tongue round her full, hungry lips and pressed her chest out at him. A brown nipple wobbled invitingly in his face, brushing his cheek and eyelids.

'Bite it ...?' There was a pleading note in her voice. Instinctively Ryan caught a nipple between his teeth, slowly squeezed it between his teeth. Her back arched, her middle pushing down onto his as though desperate to keep him still.

'F-fuck ... *fuck*!' The word came out of the depths of her throat. She hadn't come yet, but she was pursuing her climax with a ferocious determination, working her hips faster and faster. Loving him. Grinding him into the bedding.

He was close to spilling, but he restrained himself with an effort. *Just push, just keep on keeping on ...*

She came, eventually, with spasms. As if an electric current were running through her. Her back went straight and stiff and her mouth opened wide as her eyes shut.

*Say aaah-hh*, Ryan thought. Stifling an urge to giggle until the tightness of her sex around his shaft got him, made him crane upward and burst finally. She fell sideways off him, curling up and holding herself, sighing with pleasure.

Ryan lay breathing for a long while, staring at the ceiling. There was a box of tissue on the nightstand. He cleaned himself and rolled himself onto her back, arms going around her middle as though they'd been pre-programmed for that very action.

*This is what she likes, when we finish. Spooning. Me holding her. She waits for this, she loves it.*

Strange thought. He no idea why he would think such a thing, because …

'Who are you?' He whispered the word, asked her ear. 'Where'd you come from?' *Because you're wonderful?* No, that would be smarmy. Might as well ask if heaven was missing an angel.

She laughed, reached for his hand and pressed it hard against her shoulder.

'Why? You want to take me back, exchange me?'

'You know what I mean …' He tried, unsuccessfully, for a serious tone.

'No, I don't know. Tell me.' She sounded sleepy, ready to drift off. And why shouldn't she? That good old post-coital snooze, you can't beat it. *Except when you have a plane to catch at La Guardia. Except when you have a strange woman in bed with you who acts like she knows you when you've never seen her before.*

Her bare feet found his. They were icy cold. He caught them between his, thoughtlessly. Warmed them.

His eyes made a circuit of the room, viewing it more critically, his mind sharper. There were his laptop and papers, yes, and his suitcase, open but still neatly arranged. But the rest of the place, he saw now, was a disaster; shopping bags and uneaten carry-out and small piles here and there of underwear and cosmetics. Women's shoes everywhere. Many, many fashion magazines, hung on the arms of chairs or lying flat and spread open like grounded birds. The room smelled of her, a sweet mixture of perfume and skin spiced with unwashed female laundry. Like a room that had been lived in by the same woman for at least a week. But they – *he* – had only checked in yesterday. He didn't like the thought, so he pushed it from his head. He had to find out who she was.

*How do you start a conversation like this?* An unpleasant thought was occurring to Ryan, that his new friend might be crazy, or some kind of scam-artist. What other woman just gets in bed with you and pretends you're old friends?

He didn't get a chance to phrase the question. She was doing something with his hand, prising his fingers apart, looking at them. 'Where's your ring?' Her voice was concerned.

'Ring?' At the moment, the word meant nothing to him. She might have been speaking Cantonese.

'You didn't lose it? Ryan!' Panicked now. She sat up, refusing to let go of his hand.

*All right, she's crazy, then.*

'What ring?' he asked carefully.

Her eyes went wide and her mouth tightened. What would have been humour a moment ago was now sarcasm and hurt. She held up her right hand, her long fingers spread and wriggling. A plain platinum band rode on the fourth.

*Oh, my God. My God. She thinks we're married.* He had to break this to her easy. Gently. But firm as well. He had to be very firm with her.

'I ... I just took it off for a while. It was ... hurting.'

Her shoulders lowered, eyes went soft again. Mercurial. Her temper came and went. *That's why you fell in love with her*, a voice whispered to him. He ignored it.

She seized his hand, covered his fingers with soft kisses. 'I told you we would get it resized. It's not *that* much money.'

'Yeah ... yeah.' He began disengaging himself from her embrace, which was accordingly tightened.

'Where do you think you're going?'

'Just ... bathroom. Back in a minute.'

She let him go and leaned back on the covers, pouting. 'OK, but don't be long. We've both got to shower. We've got a plane to catch, don't forget. And you know what a nightmare security is these days.'

Nodding and smiling, he made his escape.

'Oh, and be careful! Your clumsy princess spilled the mouthwash.'

The small rug in the bathroom was, in fact, soaked green with mint-smelling liquid. A pair of nylons hung over the shower rod. Ryan found her wallet resting on a fat paperback behind the toilet. He tore it open and found her driver's licence.

Under her smiling, happy-looking picture was the name IRENE CARSON.

Ryan sank down onto the toilet, feeling sick. She had his last name. The DC address on the licence was his. If this was some kind of scam, it had been planned well in advance, though for what purpose he had no idea.

Fingers rapped on the door.

'Darling!' The woman's voice – *Irene's* voice – called gaily. 'Done yet? I have to tinkle!'

\* \* \*

Ryan left while she was in the shower. He moved fast, snatching up his laptop and shovelling clothes into the suitcase. He didn't stop to put on anything but jeans and a T-shirt and his running shoes.

He shut the door gently behind him, then ran for the elevator, the sound of the shower fading to nothing as he barrelled down the hallway. He'd tell the front desk that some insane woman had broken into his room. Let them deal with it. He had a plane to catch.

But as he waited for the elevator, he began feeling the plan was basically unsound. She – *Irene* – had his address. And a Washington, DC driver's licence that as good as said she was his wife.

*Do Not Disturb*

And there was the little matter of the sex. He could see the concierge nodding sympathetically, then, with an ever so slight creasing of his brow, inquire why, since Sir was so put out over the strange woman in his room, Sir had, with such evident enthusiasm, fucked her cross-eyed?

He told himself these things, but there was something else he couldn't quite escape, that he couldn't quite face.

He didn't *want* to leave her. Even though he was on the move, walking with great determination to a particular destination, the world around him seemed oppressively quiet without her sexy chatter. Less colourful without her clothes thrown everywhere. It was as though time moved more slowly without her.

Dear God, he couldn't possibly be *missing* her?

Ryan turned as the elevator opened and began walking quickly back down the hall. He would face her. Sit her down and explain the whole thing to her, even if she ended up screaming. It would be the right thing to do.

As he approached the door, he realised he couldn't hear the shower. Something was wrong. She couldn't possibly have finished so soon.

Strange thoughts fizzed up in his head like bubbles in a glass of cola. She wouldn't have finished so soon. She likes her showers. Anything with hot water. After a shower she'll fill the tub and splash around like a little girl, singing. It drives you crazy when you have a plane to catch ...

Ryan opened the door with the key-card and smelled nothing. He stepped inside, moving slowly and carefully, reminding himself of a detective. The absence of smell pervaded the entire room. No flower-scent of perfume, no sweet-stale smell of her laundry. No shoes or magazines on the floor, or loaded shopping bags. He went into the bathroom and there was no spilled mouthwash soaked into the bathroom carpet. No dog-eared romance novel, no wallet. The room was empty, without any sign of Irene Carson.

Exactly as he had left it the previous night, when he'd turned in, still single, still alone.

Ryan thought perhaps he had entered the wrong room. The solution was wonderfully appealing in its simplicity. He ran eagerly out into the hall, but the numbered plaque beside the door read 414. His room – theirs?

Either way, it was empty now, and Irene was gone.

\* \* \*

Ryan ended up missing his plane, and he didn't think that was entirely an accident on his part. He got to La Guardia in enough time to make the gate, but he couldn't seem to make himself move with any purpose.

He kept thinking about Irene. During the cab ride to the airport he had managed to convince himself that the whole episode had been some kind of elaborate hallucination. You're overworked, Carson. Seeing things. Need a vacation. By the time the cab had arrived at La Guardia he had convinced himself otherwise. He just wished he had thought to pocket her driver's licence. Even a pair of her panties.

Because women didn't just disappear, not without leaving some token of themselves behind.

At the airport Ryan finally found himself sitting outside a fast-food restaurant, staring at a couple making a display of feeding each other bites of breakfast sandwiches, snickering about it as though the whole routine was adorable. By the time they finished and left, it was too late to get to his gate. So he kept sitting. Eventually he told himself he needed to get up and at least see about getting on another flight. He could brood about Irene on the way home. He still had a job, after all. Responsibilities.

He took out his phone to call Wilson and tell him he'd be later than expected, and noticed someone had left him a voicemail. A red Number One glowing at him on the corner of phone's screen.

He accessed Voicemail with no great enthusiasm; he was sure the message would be from Wilson.

'Hello, darling. This is your clumsy princess. I'm leaving this while you're being naughty in the bathroom – at least, I assume that's what you're doing, because, without the love of a good woman ... uhm ... well. Who's to say what a good man will get up to?'

His heart was pounding. Yes, this was something she'd do. Leave little playful voicemails or texts for him when he stepped out, even if it was only to the next room. The Information Superhighway's equivalent of spontaneous love-notes.

But something was wrong with the sound. There was a strange electronic swishing noise in the background, some kind of distortion that did funny things to her voice.

'So-o-oo ... saying I *love you*. Love you and miss you ...'

The connection broke with a sudden, high-pitched whine. Ryan had a feeling the distortion had something to do with it, that Irene had actually gone on talking, unaware that she was cut off.

His heart was beating, hard and fast. Ryan wasn't a complete idiot with cell phones. He didn't know much about apps and calling plans, but he did know one thing.

He knew if someone had called and left you a voicemail, you could usually get their number from the RECENTS screen and call them right back.

Yes, and there was her number – or what must have been her number. DC area code, what a surprise. He thumbed the numerals and a small box opened up on the phone's screen, asking him if he'd like to CALL the number.

Oh, that's very good of you. How considerate. Yes, actually, I would.

## Do Not Disturb

Heart still dancing, he hit the CALL button.

It rang for ever. Every ring was a lifetime. There was more static between the rings. The electronic hissing became gradually louder, so that when she finally picked up he barely realised it.

'... Ryan ...?'

'Yes!' He was shouting into the phone, turning it in his hand so that he could speak into it from different angles and get through to her.

'... you? You're ... here ... scared ...?'

That 'scared' hit him hard. He wanted so badly for her to be there, so he could put his arms around her. He bit his lip.

*What's the matter with you? She's not married to you. You don't even know her.*

'Ry ... I want ...'

The line went dead.

Ryan's shout startled a couple walking past. He punched his thigh with frustration and the woman moved closer to the man, who gave Ryan a quick, cautious glance as he led her away.

All Ryan could think to do was get outside and try again. The signal would be stronger outside. Outside the damned thing would actually work. Reaching fresh air took a while, and as he was shouldering his way past a flock of indignant tourists, the phone rang again.

Her number.

'*Hello?*' He was desperate to hear her voice. And it came through, so clear and loud he actually shrank from the phone. As though whatever force had separated them was now taunting him with that crystal clarity.

'Ryan? Dear God, where are you?' Not panicked now, or even frightened, particularly. She sounded royally pissed off.

'I had ... I just had to go out.' *Lame. Lame, Carson.* But he had never felt so happy in his life.

'You went out ... with your *suitcase*?' She was half laughing, half ready to kill him. Ryan was laughing himself, a little hysterically.

*Wait till she hears I'm calling from La Guardia.*

'I promise ... it was this crazy thing. I'll tell you all about it. But listen, you have to ...'

Static hissed again in his ear, as though malicious forces were determined to cut them off again as quickly as possible. Ryan held the phone away, staring at it in disbelief.

*You're kidding me.*

'Ryan?' Just his name, delivered with frustration and anger and a strange plaintiveness. Then gone.

It was a fucking horror movie, he thought. She was the heroine, fading away into a strange wraith-world, an alternative dimension where they'd be so close, but never able to touch, or see each other.

The anger that rose up in him at that thought made him wanted to dash the phone onto the concrete, watch it shatter into plastic splinters. But he couldn't do that. He might need it. She might call while he was on his way back to her.

Because that's where he was going. Back to her.

Pocketing the phone, he made for the cabs.

Wilson was going to be *pissed*.

\* \* \*

The cab back to Midtown ran into traffic. Ryan sat biting his knuckles all through the ride. This is crazy, he told himself. Insane.

What was really insane, though, was how excited he was getting. Horny all over again. As the cab bumped along he kept thinking about Irene, remembering the feel of her body on his. Like he was eighteen again and a woman's touch was an unthinkable miracle. He was crazy to see her again, to feel her. He wanted to take her to bed immediately and this time explore every inch of her, from the lines on the soles of her feet to the exact shade of her hair colour. He would memorise her, not only with his eyes but with his nose and tongue. With his cock. He would imprint her on his skin, so he'd never risk losing her again.

She would be waiting for him in the room, thinking that he was only a few blocks away. She would have called by now if she had gone out to look for him. It was unthinkable that she had gone out to the airport, that they would have crossed paths on the way in separate taxis and not known it. It was *not* possible.

He made it back to the hotel somehow, finally. The girl at the check-in desk gave him a strange look that didn't last more than an eye-blink, replaced almost immediately with a smooth smile.

'Hello,' she said blithely. Blithe as all get-out. Not asking, not even thinking, *what the hell are* you *doing back here already*?

For a moment Ryan almost told the girl that his wife was still in their room and he just needed to go get her. No, that would sound *awfully* funny.

So what was he supposed to tell her? 'Excuse me, Miss. I appear to have somehow lost the woman of my dreams in a hotel in an alternate universe, so I need to get to the corresponding room in this universe because I'm sure that simple act of faith will somehow cause the universes to re-collide and deliver her back into my eager arms.'

Oh yeah, Carson. You smooth bastard. That's *much* better.

'I need a room,' he said, managing to smile but breathing heavily. He'd run in from the street. He struggled to remember which room. '414.'

'414,' she said, running her fingers over her keyboard. 'Let me just see if that's available ...'

'It has to be 414,' he said, trying desperately to sound reasonable. She had to be used to snotty corporate types making outlandish demands, wanting a room on the north side or west side, or a room with a view of the park, quite willing to bawl like infants if they weren't instantly accommodated. Surely this girl wouldn't bat an eye at him begging for a specific room.

But what if someone else had taken it? Was Irene, even now, poutingly telling some fat salesman from Bloomington, Indiana that his clumsy princess had forgotten to pick up her niece an I HEART NY T-shirt as a souvenir?

'Oh, yes ... here we are. For just the one night?'

Ryan had to stop himself from snatching the key-card from her hand. No, he didn't need help with his bags. Oh, he was sure, all right.

He ran for the elevator.

The room, when he reached it, was empty. Even emptier than last time. Housecleaning had been at it. It had a sweet, empty smell of chemicals. There was no sign of Irene. Her absence tore at him.

Ryan fell down, exhausted, onto the bed. The faith that had been in him like steel only moments ago was gone now, or turned to porridge.

He was losing his mind. No excuses this time. He was not only seeing dream-women, he was hearing their voices talking to him on his cell phone. He should consider checking himself into Bellevue while he was still in New York, assuming they'd have him.

Self-pity and fear for his sanity gradually gave way to a feeling of emptiness. It was a strangely gentle feeling. Everyone in the world felt like this eventually, didn't they? Sure they did. They wanted something or someone more than anything, and they couldn't get it/them, no matter how hard they tried.

Ryan lay watching bars of sunlight track slowly across the ceiling. He didn't want to ever move again. The stress of the past few hours began catching up with him, demanding he relax his muscles, showing him how good it would be to shut his eyes, just for a minute. Sleep stole up on him eventually. He didn't fight it.

He woke up like diving through a bank of cottony clouds into sweetness. The room smelled sweet, like her perfume, like her laundry and the syrup-filled chocolates she liked to snack on in bed. He felt weight on his legs. Irene was there, lying on top of him, barefoot in a sundress. Her nails were freshly done, a maroon that went beautifully with her skin tone.

She had unzipped him, taken his cock out and was holding it, lapping at it like an ice-cream cone.

'Where the hell were you?' she whispered, her lips moving over his pink head as if she were speaking into a microphone. Her eyes were fixed on his, unreadable. 'I looked and looked. We missed our plane. This is your punishment.'

She licked his cockhead again and he shuddered at the intensity of the feeling. No more emptiness. Joy was back instead, so strong he didn't have the strength to cry out or grab her. He lay back with his eyes shut, smiling idiotically. *I'm crazy, but I don't care. I don't.*

'I'm not going away again,' he told her. 'I promise. If I go anywhere, you're coming with me.' *For the rest of our lives. I'm never losing you again.*

'You're right about *that*, Mr Man. And look ...' She gave his cock a last kiss, climbed up so they were cheek to cheek. She took his hand and slipped something over the fourth finger. 'There,' she said smiling.

'What?' he asked, but he knew what it was. He held his hand up. Late-afternoon sunlight caught the metal and gleamed. It looked strangely familiar now.

Irene bit his earlobe. 'I found your ring,' she told him.

## Ice Is Nice
## Louise Hooker

'*This* is what you chose?' Caroline said, setting her bags down on the snow-covered floor.

The place was beautiful, without a doubt, but it was definitely not what Caroline had expected her husband to pick for their getaway. She had been expecting Vegas, California, New York ... not Canada. Not that Canada was not nice, agatin. And even less expected than Canada was the ice hotel she was now standing in, shivering. She glanced down at her brown luggage set, furrowing her brow as she wondered if it was cold enough for her bags to freeze to the floor. Then she brought her eyes back up to the room her husband Victor had rented for a couple of nights' time. It was definitely a suite. It had just about everything you could expect from just a standard room, the little table with two club chairs, a bed, a chest of drawers – except ... it was all carved out of snow and

## Do Not Disturb

friggin' *ice*. A fireplace, unlit, stood in one corner of the room. Caroline approached the bed, sat down on the only non-ice thing she had seen in the place aside from the fireplace – the comforter and pillow set – and was pleasantly surprised to find that the mattress was just an ordinary mattress. She sighed in relief. Victor laughed at her.

'You didn't *really* think they'd make people sleep on a block of ice? That could kill you,' he said, picking up her discarded bags and moving them to an out-of-the-way corner of the room.

Caroline did not even crack a smile. 'I didn't know what to expect.'

Victor crossed his arms over his broad chest – honestly, the first thing Caroline had noticed on him, next to his brilliant green eyes, those five years ago when they had met at a mutual friend's wedding.

'You said that we couldn't mock the other one's choices, and that I got to pick the hotel,' he reminded her.

Caroline nodded. It was very true. Those had been her terms. They would be married five years, exactly, come three days from now, but that marriage was … well, on ice. They had tried for children a couple of years back, and somewhere along the way, with all the ovulation sticks, pregnancy tests and fertility-doctor visits, they had grown mute. Once upon a time, they always had something to say to one another, even on a boring day.

Used to be, they would miss each other if they went more than a day without being in the same room, and their lovemaking ... oh, the lovemaking. But all of that was gone now. They had become comfortable with each other in the worst way, resorting to living like roommates more than husband and wife. They still loved each other, though. Or, at least, that was what this trip was setting out to discover. Could they save their marriage by a simple getaway where they let loose, forgetting their normal, everyday concerns ... or would they have to seek professional help? Or worse?

'I'd pick the hotel, wherever, whatever, and you would pick the kink, so long as it wasn't borderline illegal. No questions asked, and the other would go along. That was *your* idea, Caroline,' Victor reiterated, not moving one muscle to sit beside his wife.

Caroline nodded, pushing the furred hood of her heavy coat off her head to reveal her dark brunette hair. She ran a gloved hand through her locks, shaking them out and down until they fell to their natural length – about midway down her small torso. She smiled up at Victor, nodding again. She stood and moved to wrap her arms about him, as best she could with his broadness and his own heavy blue winter coat not really aiding her.

'I know. It was just ... I decided my kink and I'm just a little worried about doing it here. I'm not sure how sexy it'll be if my teeth are clattering,' she laughed.

Victor smiled down at her, his green eyes finding her brown ones. She knew that look, and it was such a relief to see it again. That mischievous glance that was teasing her, having fun with her. It relaxed Caroline instantly to see it, like an old friend, and she tightened her hug.

'So ... what did you choose?' Victor asked, bending to brush her ear with his lips.

She *loved* that. She shivered, and not from the cold, and shook her head. She backed away, placing a finger of her glove to his lips.

'Nu-uh,' she said, giggling. 'Remember? It's a secret until it's time for us to do it.'

Victor laughed, picked her up like she weighed nothing and carried her to the bed. He leaned over her – his six and a half feet of height impressive to her five and one inch – covering her completely. He planted a kiss on her lips, deep and full, and it felt like the most natural thing in the world. Like all their marital problems had just *poofed* into thin air. He pulled back and unzipped her coat just a little so that he could lean in and nibble on her neck. She moaned, her hips grinding up into him.

'What's stopping us from doing it now?' he murmured into her skin.

Oh, wow, was *that* tempting. Where was *this* Victor back at home? His voice was deep, guttural, like he would take her now, no matter her protests. And she kind of liked that. But she resisted, no matter how warm her body had suddenly gotten – which was a welcome relief from the cold she was not used to – and gently pushed her husband up.

'Nope. We made the mutual agreement that we would spend a romantic, non-sexual evening together. Drinks, dinner, fun. And then sex. That was part of the plan,' she said.

Victor laughed. 'If it's leading to sex, how can it be non-sexual?'

Caroline considered that for a moment. Finally, she shrugged.

'I just mean, no pawing or groping while we're out. Just kisses, hugs, dancing, talking, wine, song. You know.'

Victor got back to his feet, and, even through the thick denim that he wore, Caroline could see the familiar bulge of his arousal. It pleased her to know that it was not a rush, there was nothing at stake here – well, save their marriage. But they were not going to make love with the agenda of procreation. It was going to happen naturally. At that thought, her eyes flew to her suitcase, and she bit her lip lightly. She *really* hoped what she had picked for their new kink was not going to be too silly. Nothing killed the mood like being laughed at.

Victor held out a hand and pulled her to her feet. Once he let go, he handed her a pamphlet, and she took it with a brow raised. As she began to unfold it, he ran a hand over his short blond hair – very short, almost shaved – and Caroline vaguely wondered how his head was not freezing.

'It's a list of the attractions and stuff they have here. There's a bar, a slide ... all kinds of stuff. Oh, and you can even take the tour and learn more about its construction and stuff. I know you like tours and crap.'

Caroline laughed, and he gave her a questioning look. She shook her head, her eyes flitting back down to the section of the pamphlet about the bar.

'I want to do stuff we'll *both* enjoy. This trip is about *us*, not you and me separate, you know?'

He wrapped an arm about her shoulders. 'Yeah. And, what, five minutes in, and we're doing OK? Right?'

She breathed in deeply, ignoring the fact that frigid temperatures made her nostrils hurt. She leaned her head on his shoulder – or, at least, as close as she could get to his shoulder – and nodded.

'Yeah. Honestly, I do feel better.'

'That's good, right?'

'I'd like to think so.'

Victor smiled like he had accomplished some grand quest. He pointed towards the door of their room and gently guided her towards it.

'Then let's have some fun, shall we?'

Caroline nodded. 'OK. But let's hit the bar first ... I think I could use something warming.'

Victor nodded. 'I agree. Of course, we could just go

into the spa that's attached to this room if we get cold tonight.'

He pointed to a darkened doorway that Caroline had somehow managed to miss in her original scan of the room. Her eyes widened.

'Is *that* why you told me to pack a bathing suit?'

\* \* \*

Caroline had to admit, the bar was cool, and this time she was not speaking just of the temperature. They both ordered simple alcoholic beverages to begin with, nothing complicated, and marvelled at the bartender mixing them inside square glasses with a circular centre that were made entirely of ice. To the right of the bar was a fireplace, with clear ice benches surrounding it in a square, while secluded corner booths carved into the walls were behind them and to the left. They chose one of the booths.

She slid in first, followed by Victor boxing her in, and they clinked their cubic ice glasses together before downing the beverage within. The burn of the alcohol was warming all the way down to her stomach, and she instantly felt her body relax.

'So far so good,' Victor said, setting his glass down.

'I wish you'd stop doing that,' Caroline said.

He turned to her. 'Doing what?'

'Counting down the fun. Or counting up. Or whatever

the hell it is with you always mentioning that we're doing good.'

'But we are. I just want this to work. Is that so bad?'

She shook her head. 'Of course not. But it's feeling forced. Like you're afraid I'm going to explode at you or something.'

'Well, you didn't seem too happy with the hotel I picked, even though I got the best suite they have here. That was a *private* spa, by the way.'

She turned to stare at her husband, somewhere between being pleased that he had really worked hard to pick the best of what he wanted for his portion of their deal and being pissed that he was just assuming that she was angry with him. She chose to go with a middle ground – soft annoyance.

'I'm not angry,' she huffed. 'I was just worried about whether my kink would work here or not. Or whether we'd actually get to have sex in this climate. But I am pleased with your choice. It's really exotic. Nothing like what we usually do.'

'You mean, our usual fifty-dollar-a-night cheap hotel where you're left wondering how many prostitutes have slept on the bed before you?' he chuckled.

She laughed, nodding. 'Exactly.'

He lifted his empty glass as if toasting. 'Mission accomplished!'

She clapped a hand over her mouth to keep her laughter

in check, and didn't remove it until it was reduced to giggles. She sighed, snuggling up to her husband.

'Let's just talk. We haven't just talked in a while,' she said.

'I thought we were talking.'

She looked up at him, about to snap, when she saw that look again. That playful tease that told her that he was just being silly. She smiled and returned his playfulness with a slap across the arm.

'You know what I mean,' she said, grin still in place.

He nodded. 'All right, what do you want to talk about?'

Caroline did not answer, searching her mind. What did she want to talk about? She wanted to avoid the subject of their marriage as much as possible. This was about that, but it was also about getting away from those troubles to see if this trip could fix it. She wanted to think about relaxing things, and, hopefully, what the night would bring for them. She gazed up at the man she had been with for the last five years, and her heart broke a little that she felt as if she had nothing to say to him. What could that mean? Surely nothing good. But Victor smiled down at her.

'I've got an idea,' he said. 'Let's do a survey.'

'A survey?' she asked, her voice deadpan.

'Yeah. Like we did on our first date.'

Caroline's heart swelled. He remembered that? On

## Do Not Disturb

their first date, in a nice, cosy Italian restaurant, both had confessed that – away from other people, like the situation they had met in – they were both rather shy. So, to break the ice, Caroline had suggested that they ask each other twenty questions about anything. The other would answer as honestly as possible, no matter what the consequences. They had shaken on it, sealing the deal to be honest with each other for the first time ever. Now, she nodded.

'OK. Let's do it. You go first. Are we doing twenty apiece?'

'Let's take it slow. Five apiece,' he said.

Five. She could come up with five, easy. So she nodded, and Victor took a moment to think. Finally, he grinned.

'What's the dirtiest fantasy you've ever had? And I won't take offence if it didn't involve me.'

Caroline blushed. He was really going no-holds-barred.

'Um, this was supposed to be non-sexual,' she muttered.

Victor shrugged. 'Doesn't matter.'

'OK, we're doing our honesty thing, right?'

He held out his hand, and she locked gloves with him and shook. She laughed once, nervously, and continued.

'A threesome.'

He arched a brow. 'A threesome? Two girls and one guy, or two guys one girl?'

Victor had always been the brazen one. The first to suggest new things to try in the bedroom, while Caroline had always planned the day-to-day stuff, hence the reason she had chosen to pick the kink to try. New things could be good for character building, she had heard.

'Both.' She blushed.

Victor's eyes widened. 'I'll keep that in mind. Your turn.'

'Well, since you asked a sex question, then *I'll* ask one,' she said as if she had been challenged. 'Where's the most daring place you've ever come at?'

'Like, physical place?'

She nodded.

'OK. I once masturbated in a public restroom stall. Not my proudest moment, but it was kind of exhilarating too.'

The thought of it made a flush of heat run through Caroline's body, and apparently it showed. Victor smiled at her, pulling her even closer. He leaned down and kissed the lobe of her ear.

'Wanna go back to the room?'

Caroline fidgeted, and she could feel herself growing ready for him. She had not wanted to rush through the romantic portion of their getaway. But her body was practically itching. She thought for a moment, a single moment, and decided that she wasn't going to fight instinct. She nodded.

'Let's go.'

\* \* \*

## Do Not Disturb

They were in the spa adjoining their room, and it was warm. Deliciously warm. A bubbling hot tub stood in the middle, with a carved ice bench, much like the ones that had surrounded the fireplace in the bar, running the length of the left wall. A set of wooden steps led up to the mouth of the tub, and Victor was already inside. Caroline had instructed him to shut his eyes, since she had to change – it was part of the kink. He had smiled and complied.

Now, Caroline ignored her one-piece bathing suit, digging past it in the suitcase to a plastic garment bag, much like the one Halloween costumes are sold in. She checked to make sure Victor's eyes were still shut, and then slipped out of everything she was wearing – coat, clothes and underwear. Then she opened the bag with a snap, and she watched as Victor's brow twitched upwards. She was breathing heavily as she withdrew the lacy garment, untangling it so that it dangled in front of her.

It was one piece, going from feet to neck. It slipped on like a full body stocking and was pitch-black lace. She pulled it over her pale flesh, noting how the crotchlessness of it was not as odd to her as she had expected it to be. It had a keyhole cut right over her taut stomach, with the rest of the lacy garment wrapping around her back and covering her breasts. It had a single collar, layered thicker than the rest, that slipped over her head to hold the entire outfit up, but Caroline was not to be satisfied with just that. She reached into the plastic bag and withdrew an item she had purchased separately – a black collar with attached leash. In solid silver letters around the front, it read 'slave'. She snapped it in place, trailing the chain leash out so that the handle was easily within her husband's reach. Careful not to yank it to the floor, she posed as best she could, resisting the urge to cover herself. She placed her hands on her hips, holding them there so tightly that it seemed as if they had a mind of their own.

'I thought we'd try role-playing,' she said. 'Open your eyes.'

Victor's eyes slid open, and, based on the look he swept her body with, she imagined that his member hardened just as fast.

'Role-playing?' he asked.

She gestured to the handle of the leash. 'I'm your slave. I'll do whatever you say, Master.'

She felt ridiculous. The best she was hoping for at the moment was that Victor would not die of laughter. But her husband took up the handle and tugged it, hard enough to jerk her into the side of the hot tub.

'Yes, you will,' he said.

Caroline felt a thrill of electricity run through her body, and she moaned. Victor smiled at her, nodding his head towards the steps.

'Get in,' he ordered.

She nodded, but he yanked on her chain, forcing her to fold over the mouth of the tub.

'Answer me when I speak to you.'

He was really into this, and Caroline grinned. She looked up at him from under her eyelashes.

'Yes, Master.'

She climbed the steps to the tub and lowered herself gingerly into it. The water was hot, hotter than she had expected, and she had practically no covering on her skin. She hissed at it, but continued to work her way down. When the warmth hit her nether regions, she sighed, pleased at the tingle it gave her. She moved to sit on the inner bench of the tub across from Victor, the chain providing more than enough leeway. Her husband cocked his head to the side.

'You've already got me hard,' he noted in a voice so gruff that it told Caroline that he had not broken character.

She glanced through the clear water, surprised to find Victor's familiar Hawaiian-print trunks missing. Instead, a full and erect cock peered up at her, its already ample thickness and length amplified by the water. Caroline's pussy was growing warmer by the minute, water aside.

'What shall I do for you, Master?' she asked, in her best innocent tones.

Victor eyed her for a moment, clearly in debate. Finally,

he lay back, switched the handle of her leash from his right hand to his left and wrapped his now free hand around his dick.

'Touch yourself.'

Caroline hesitated. She was no saint – masturbation was not foreign to her. But putting a hand to her pussy without her husband already inside her was something that she had always felt a little strange about when he was watching. He tugged the chain, bringing her forwards so that he caught her about the neck.

'Are you disobeying me?' he demanded.

The growl in his voice made her shiver in all the right places, and she shook her head, playing fearful.

'No, Master!'

He shoved her back against the other side of the tub. She landed a little harder than necessary, and a flicker of concern crossed her husband's face. She smiled at him, and he relaxed, slipping back into his role.

'Then do it.'

She lifted her feet up to rest on either side of him. He grinned, his hand slowly moving up and down his member. She raised a hand and, starting just above her breasts, slid it down her body as slowly as she could. Victor's lips parted and his breathing grew heavy. His tongue snaked out as she crossed her abdomen, her fingers beginning to slither down to that heavenly bundle of nerves at the top of her opening. The pad of her index finger touched her clitoris, and she moaned, moving the finger slowly in a circle. Victor's stroking grew faster and harder as he watched.

'That's it,' he gasped. 'Faster.'

She obeyed, moving the finger faster and faster, feeling her clit tighten as her arousal grew. Her left hand glided up the side of her body, cupped her breast and massaged it. She let her fingers dance across her taut nipple, the texture of the lace an interesting new discovery as she worked her fingers harder and harder on her clit.

'Finger yourself,' Victor ordered.

This time, she did not think twice. She moved her hand down and inserted a single finger inside her slit. She fucked herself slowly at first, meanwhile sliding her left hand across one breast to the other.

'God, yes,' Victor moaned.

'Do you like this, Master?' she whispered.

He nodded, letting go of his cock to cup and rub his balls. He let her fuck herself a while longer, and Caroline felt the heat growing in her body, moving closer and closer to coming. Finally, he took his hands off himself and tugged on the chain.

'Enough.'

She stopped, sliding the finger out with a gasp. Her hands dropped below the water to grip the bench she sat on. Her legs, still spread either side of her husband, were quaking. Now Victor moved so that he sat out of the tub, his ass balanced on its edge. Caroline noted how his dick broke through the water magnificently as he tugged her forwards.

'Suck me,' he said.

Now was time to have a little fun, to see how committed Victor was to his role. Caroline struggled against the leash, trying to sit back upon her bench.

'But, I can't possibly fit that whole dick in my mouth,' she argued.

'Do it *now*,' he said.

But she shook her head, still fighting. Victor huffed, wrapped the chain about his hand once and gave it a mighty tug. She all but flew across the water, and he caught her by the head just as he had before. This time, however, his hand wound itself up in her hair.

'I said, suck,' he said, forcing his dick into her mouth.

There was no working up to it. He forced it all the way in to the hilt. She gagged once, unprepared, but he removed it a moment later. He grinned down at her, a light dancing in his eyes.

'Actually, I have a better idea,' he said.

Without letting go of the chain, he held her head in both hands and forced his cock back inside her mouth. This time she had been expecting it, so she allowed her tongue to tickle the shaft. He pulled it back out, then repeated the motion, faster and faster, fucking her mouth.

'Ah, yes, yes!' he moaned as Caroline got increasingly

better at letting her tongue do its work in the short time it had with each thrust.

She realised her hands were unoccupied, and so she reached up to cup and stroke his balls. He groaned, thrusting even harder. Her pussy ached, desperate for relief. She had never seen Victor like this before, so intense … so carnal. He had always been a passionate lover who was good at what he did, but this was something new. He was not just enjoying this role-playing, he was *loving* it. And that excited Caroline more than she would have ever thought possible. Keeping one hand on his balls, she moved the other down to her slit. However, before she could even begin to give herself any relief, Victor shoved her head back, her mouth so close, but so far away, from the cock she greatly wanted to be sucking. He brushed the head against her lips, but did not let it part them.

'No, no. I didn't say you could touch yourself,' he said.

Her hands flew back up and gripped the bench in front of her.

'I'm sorry, Master. I didn't know. Please, *please* let me suck your dick,' she pleaded.

'No. That's twice that you've been bad. Only good little slaves get to suck,' he said.

He moved her back, careful to still keep her close to him, as he sat back down in the water.

She batted her eyes at him. 'Are you going to punish me?'

'Yes,' he said.

She turned and stuck out her ass. They had spanked before, outside role-playing, and it was something she had found she quite enjoyed. So she was ready for it, and her buttocks tensed as she felt her husband caress them.

'I've been bad, Master. Punish me,' she whispered.

She could almost imagine the wicked grin on Victor's face.

'Don't worry, I will. But I think I'm going to try something new.'

A look of panic crossed Caroline's features, and she was about to ask him exactly what he meant by that. But, before she could, she felt him move his pinkie finger up the crack of her ass.

'Just a small one, because you haven't been horribly bad,' he said.

Caroline struggled, entirely independent from her character. She tried to get away, but her husband had a tight grip on her hips.

'No,' she moaned, but Victor didn't listen.

He shoved his finger inside her ass, and she clenched at the foreign feeling. He wiggled his finger and she gasped.

'Please, please ... I can't.'

'You can, and you will. You've been bad,' he said, moving the pinkie in and out of her. 'Might as well enjoy me finger-fucking your ass. Maybe you won't disobey me next time.'

## Do Not Disturb

He was moving slowly, but Caroline could feel him picking up momentum. Her ass remained clenched, and a hot blush coloured her from head to toe. He had never played with her ass like this before. The single time before this that they had tried it, she had stopped him at the head of his dick. She just could not take it, feeling his rock-hard cock spreading her ass wide open. But this ... this was not entirely unpleasant. Foreign, uncharted and odd, yes ... but not bad. She moaned, her body tugging at the grip he still had on her hips. He laughed.

'You like this, don't you?'

She nodded, unable to speak. But Victor understood. He wrapped his free arm about her waist and twisted his hand until his rough finger pressed down on her clit. He rubbed at it just as ferociously as his pinkie was now fucking her ass. Caroline moaned, bucking her hips back to meet each thrust.

'I think I want you to come like this,' he said, rubbing her clit faster.

The rhythms of his movements were matching and accelerating. Heat was building up in Caroline's pussy, and it was not going to be long before it exploded to the rest of her body.

'Yes, Master,' she moaned, her eyes tightly shut. 'Fuck my ass. I'm so close!'

'Yes,' Victor growled, his grip about her waist vice-like.

She was on the edge now, and was practically screaming

with the frustration. Vaguely, she wondered if the other hotel visitors could hear them, fucking away in their private spa. In the end, however, she just did not care. Victor pressed down a little harder on her clit, while still thrusting his pinkie in and out of her asshole. It was too much, and Caroline cried out, the wave of orgasm washing over her body. She collapsed over Victor's arm, limp. He removed his pinkie while she gasped, and turned her around to face him.

'Good girl,' he said.

He reached up and unclasped her collar for just a moment while he slipped the lace up over her head. Then he ran his tongue from her navel to her neck. She moaned, tossing her head back. He pulled down on the chain, hard, and her freshly wet pussy slid over his cock without a hitch. She gasped, feeling so filled, as she fell against his chest. He bit down on her neck, and her hips bucked. He moaned and moved his mouth down to suck one of her breasts. He flicked his tongue across the erect nipple, and Caroline began to sway back and forth on his rock-hard member.

Victor pulled back, gazing up at her. 'Now, fuck me like a good slave.'

He moved one of her hands down between them, and Caroline knew what he meant. She placed one finger on her sensitive clit, jumping at the touch, and began to ride her husband like she never had before. Victor leaned forwards, kissing and licking each of her breasts in turn, flicking his tongue across her nipples as Caroline rode harder and harder. His dick was hitting all the right places, her clit beginning to grow tight again as she rubbed her finger across it.

'Yeah, fuck me like that. Good girl,' Victor groaned, his hands wrapped tightly around her back.

Caroline rode him with all her might, shoving her pussy down as hard as she could with each thrust, gasping and moaning as she did. She was getting close again, and one of Victor's hands slid up to grasp the nape of her neck.

Her eyes opened – she did not know when she had shut them – and found Victor's. Suddenly, a new feeling filled her. He gazed up at her, and they held that look. Suddenly, everything was clear. This marriage, them … it was worth saving. She loved Victor with all her might, and she never wanted to let him go. She wondered if he was feeling the same way.

As if reading her thoughts, he leaned forward and planted a chaste kiss on her collarbone – too chaste for the way she was riding him now. But it was just right, just enough. A moment later, without any warning, her body drove over the edge. She gasped, feeling her pussy tighten around his cock as she forced her hips to keep moving through the orgasm. Victor, using the leash, pulled her forwards and embraced her body. Caroline's pussy was twitching, convulsing with the pleasure that filled her. A moment later, she heard Victor's strangled cry of joy, his lips pressed to her neck, as he spilled inside her. Spent, she pulled herself off his dick and sat beside him. For a long while they simply sat there, their gasps the only sound between them. Finally, Victor chuckled.

'Role-playing,' he said.

She nodded.

'Slave girl.'

She nodded again.

'Can we keep this kink?'

She smiled. 'If you want.'

He turned, taking both her hands in his. 'For ever and ever.'

Something told her that the kink was not what he was talking about now. She leaned against him, hugging him tight.

'For ever and ever,' she agreed.

# *Flashing*
## Rachel Kramer Bussel

It wasn't my idea to accept the all-expenses paid trip to Honolulu, but my husband, Connor, insisted. 'You can't turn down an amazing opportunity like that.'

'But what's the point of lying around at a beach resort when you won't be there with me?' Don't get me wrong – I'm not incapable of travelling alone; I do it frequently for my job as a food and travel writer. But I'd just wrapped up a stint of back-to-back trips, and in the two weeks I'd been home Connor had been busy with end-of-year reports, and I'd been looking forward to spending a sexy New Year's Eve with him. I'm not usually sentimental about holidays – we don't celebrate Valentine's Day or Christmas – but New Year's is a particular favourite of mine. It's also our anniversary, picked specifically because we'd assumed that any boss in the world would understand the need for a day off to celebrate the ushering in of a new year, and the fact that the world is usually celebrating with us. We often travel, and have woken up to start new years together all over the globe, from Paris to Reykjavik to Dubai to Mexico City.

I'd discovered, though, that things were different when you became your own boss. I had staff jobs for a long time and, if I couldn't go on a particular trip, someone else could easily fill in, and we found ways of juggling the choice assignments so everyone's needs were accommodated.

Of course, I could say no; legally, nobody was stopping me. But not only did I worry about the karmic implications of turning down such a luxurious free ride, I also knew that the travel agency arranging it could find plenty of other people more than willing, able and eager to hop on a plane on a moment's notice for the chance to bask in five-star comfort. I love hotels, too, which is part of what led me to this job, but I love my husband even more and had been particularly hungry for him the past few weeks. My fantasies had been less about room service and more about turning off our cell phones, locking our bedroom door and getting reacquainted with every inch of each other's body. All we'd managed lately were quickies that left me wanting more every time. I came, and so did he, but that wasn't enough. I craved the kind of intense lovemaking that left you sore, breathless, trembling and weak; that consumed you for so long you forgot about everything else in the world.

## Do Not Disturb

I'd found myself seeing phallic objects everywhere, making typos and misreading words in some kind of twisted sexual dyslexia, with everything reminding me of Connor and how hot it was to slip between the sheets with him. Six years isn't a milestone anniversary, but to me it was a big deal, and I'd planned to bake him his favourite double chocolate brownies stark naked in our kitchen, with plenty of extra batter for him to lick off me.

'Honey, you know I want to spend our anniversary with you, but I can't in good conscience encourage you to turn down an opportunity like this. It's what you've been working towards all this time, getting your name known and recognised as the hotshot we both know you are. I have a feeling that next year we're going to see your byline in the *New York Times*, and I know you'll take me with you when you can. We can celebrate extra when you get home. And actually, well, maybe we can still celebrate in bed.'

'What do you mean?'

'I mean Skype,' he said, as if it were the most natural thing in the world. 'I mean I want a free hot sexy peepshow, and I want you to do anything I tell you to. Isn't that what technology is for?' He pulled me towards him, and I felt exactly how hard this discussion was making him.

'But what's the point if we can't touch each other?' I whined, wrapping my hand around his erection to prove my point.

'I guess you'll find out,' he said, and dragged my mouth towards him for a passionate kiss. I usually stand on my tiptoes to reach him, but this time Connor lifted me up onto the counter, pressed his hand against the back of my head and slammed my mouth against his. His tongue entered my mouth and claimed every inch of it. When I was utterly breathless, he whispered in my ear, 'Just make sure you don't get too sunburned or tire yourself out because you are going to be my personal little porn star. Maybe I'll even invite some friends over to watch you, guys you don't know, from the office. I'm always telling them how fucking sexy you are but they don't know the half of it.' I knew it was just talk, but it was talk that made me very, very wet.

I pushed my skirt down and soon was sitting there bare, while my husband sucked on my nipples. He pulled my body to the edge of the counter and started stroking me as he continued. 'Maybe I'll get them to make suggestions about what they want to see you do. Most of them are always telling me about how they only fuck a few times a month, so I bet they have plenty of ideas about what you can put right here.' With that, he plunged two fingers inside me. 'Put your fingers in your mouth, Farrah, and suck them like you're going to do when I show you off. I want them to see how good a cocksucker you are. Maybe if you do a really good job, I'll invite one of them back and watch you take his dick down your

## Do Not Disturb

throat.' I was sobbing around my extremely wet fingers, right there with Connor as he spun his fantasy. I love my husband desperately, love every inch of his incredible body, especially his cock, but I had always had a fantasy, hidden from every lover but him, of taking two cocks in my mouth at once. I'd wondered if I could do it, or if I'd alternate, getting one nice and wet, then the other. In my head, I'd played out pretty much everything a girl could do with two dicks at once, but all I'd told him was the dual-blowjob part of my secret turn-on.

Picturing him in the same room with another man who was turned on watching me get naked was overkill, and I shuddered, clenching my teeth and breathing fiercely as I clutched the counter and came. Connor's fingers finally emerged, wet and wrinkled, and he fed them to me. I pulled them slowly into my mouth, savouring his skin and my juices, and the promise he was offering me. He eased me down, turned me around and entered me from behind, pumping into me in deep, long strokes. I climaxed again soon after he did, the rush of it all making me gasp.

I fell asleep long before dinner, woke up at 3 a.m. and curled myself around Connor's body for a while. Then I wearily packed my skimpiest beachwear, a black-and-white polka-dot one-piece, a basic navy racerback, a hot pink bikini and a little red number complete with a tennis-style skirt and well-supported top. I didn't really care; I was blissed out on the afterglow and rode it all the way until I settled into my first-class seat.

\* \* \*

I arrived in Honolulu on a steamy evening, awed by the thickness of the heat and the life pulsing along Kalakaua Avenue as my taxi made its way to the hotel. During my first trip, I'd rented a room from a local, near the beach in Waikiki, where I could walk to get an acai bowl before spending the afternoon baking under the sun or learning how to surf. This time, though, I was getting special treatment, and I couldn't wait to sink into the plush bed I'd been promised. When I checked in, I found out that, because someone else couldn't make it, I was being upgraded to a private, secret suite, tucked away in a far corner. Upon opening the door, I was shocked. The suite was easily twice the size of our apartment back home, suitable for many guests, gluttony for one. I was tempted to splurge on a last-minute ticket for Connor, but I knew he had responsibilities too.

Instead, I explored the room, amazed again and again at the sumptuousness at my fingertips. The thread count on the sheets was higher than any I'd ever slept on, while the flat-screen TV took up practically a whole wall. Complimentary champagne came in three different vintages, and the free custom minibar featured everything

## Do Not Disturb

from triple cream Brillat-Savarin Brie to a variety of chocolate truffles. Room service was complimentary, the leather-bound menu merely offering 'suggestions'. We were free to order whatever we liked and, as long as the staff had the ingredients on hand, they'd send it up.

I was told all I had to do was press a button and someone would be there to greet me. As soon as I was alone, the first thing I did was the first thing I always do in a hotel room: get naked. I usually wear a silk robe at home, but something about being in a hotel always makes me want to stay as close to my birthday suit as I can. I checked myself out in the mirror, turned on the radio and twirled around the room, dancing and laughing until I collapsed on the bed. Then a pang hit me: as gorgeous as this free luxury was, I missed the one man who could make it even better. I reached for my suitcase, figuring I could journal about it, then head out for a drink. Inside, though, I found two elegant red velvet pouches I was sure I hadn't packed.

Inside the first was a Post-It note. 'Something to remember me by,' was scrawled in Connor's almost indecipherable handwriting, which had taken me at least two years to figure out. Inside was a brand-new Purple Rabbit vibrator, along with batteries. In the other pouch I found a light-blue butt plug, a small bottle of lube and nipple clamps with tiny bells attached to the ends that jingled as I moved them around, along with another note he'd taken care to write in big block letters: USE ONLY WITH ME. Clearly, the 'with' in that order was a virtual one, but I knew that, with Connor, watching was almost as good as being there. I smiled to myself as I fingered the toys, feeling connected to him even from so many miles away. Maybe if my career took off we could come back here together.

I put the toys back in their pouches, lest I be tempted to use them. Connor would know for sure, because I have no semblance of a poker face, and because I'd surely want to tell him about it. We didn't own a pair of nipple clamps, because his teeth and fingers had done such a good job all these years, but my nipples were definitely among the most sensitive parts of my body. From what I could remember, though, I'd always needed a lover's steady hand to guide them. Just thinking about that, not to mention the fact that Connor had planned such a sneaky surprise, had me so horny I couldn't wait for him. He'd be sleeping, and it wasn't worth waking him just now.

Instead I drew myself a bath and took out the one sex toy I always carry with me, because you never know – a small waterproof vibrator that had seen me through many trips and adventures. I'd used it while showering outdoors with Connor, in a bathroom stall during an eight-hour unexpected airport layover, and in my own bedroom. It was a standby, one my body was as attuned to as to any

## Do Not Disturb

lover. I admired my choice of bubble-bath scents: vanilla, strawberry and lavender. Vanilla has always smelled like sex to me, so I chose that, along with an ice-cold bottle of Coke and some M&Ms from the mini fridge, and soon the sumptuous bathroom, far too big for one person, was sweetly scented. I slid into the marble bathtub, resting my head against the sloping side as the bubbles washed over me. I sipped my drink, the chill a welcome contrast to the hot-as-I-could stand water. Normally I watch what I eat, but when I'm at a hotel I let go in every way. Connor and I have had some of our hottest sexual escapades in hotels, and I thought about the threesome in Belize as I reached under the water and began to touch myself.

As it turned out, I didn't even need the vibrator, but I was grateful it was handy. My biggest turn-on ever is, clichéd as it may sound, Connor. Hearing him talk to me, telling me anything – that I'm his special little slut, that he wants me to do the most depraved things you can imagine, that he wants to kiss me until we can't breathe – sets me off like nothing else. In lieu of that, I spoke to myself, pretending alternately that I was a queen with manservants waiting at the ready to service me, and that the tub was empty and those same servants were in fact my captors and were going to come all over me. That's what did it – blasting the water down onto me and pretending it was really the anonymous men's come. I barely made it out of the tub and into bed, but when I did I crashed hard, lulled into the beauty of post-orgasmic sleep.

\* \* \*

The next morning I woke up to a blaring cell phone. Connor had been calling me, and, though I was sleepy, I quickly woke up when I heard his sexy voice in my ear. 'You're still in bed?' he asked with a hint of arousal, enough to make me stop longing for the luxury of sleep, enough to wake up my clit and tell him all about what I got up to in the bathroom the night before.

'Did you get my present? You didn't thank me.' He didn't sound upset, more mock annoyed, the tone he gets when he's looking for a reason to take me over his knee and give me a spanking. Sometimes he's *too* good an actor, and I can't actually tell whether he's upset or giving me grief, but this time I was sure. We don't need the pretence of punishment, but we both like it.

'I like it, baby,' I murmured, slowly waking up, happy to hear from him but with a slight pang that all I could do was hear and not touch him. My favourite times with him are lazy mornings when nobody needs our urgent attention and we can spend hours kissing and entwining and eating and then starting all over again. It's not as much fun on my own, but perhaps that's about to change, because Connor told me, 'Why don't you show me how much you like it? I've been thinking about seeing you wearing those clamps and how pretty the butt plug would look in your ass. It's made me very hard. I want you to hang up the phone, set up your laptop and get your ass ready to show me you putting it in.'

I flushed, even though he couldn't see me yet. It's one thing to wear a butt plug, but to have him watch me put it in? That was a whole other thing. I'd never done that before; he was always the one who'd penetrated me, who'd held me open and made me aware of just how much I like to be played with there. I never did, before him. I could handle a finger if the guy I was with really wanted to give me one, but it didn't do anything for me, not the way I'd seen women in porn go crazy, or even the way the guys who let me do it to them went crazy. But with Connor my backdoor was as sensitive as any other erogenous zone. The first time, he had me take a bath, then knelt at the edge of the tub and licked me back there until I begged to touch myself. From there, we moved on to his fingers coated with lube, various sizes of butt plugs, and his cock, usually with a vibrator whirring against my pussy or clit – or both!

So many images of him stroking me there flashed through my mind as I hung up on our call, got out my laptop, logged into Skype and checked out my ass in the mirror on the wall. It would be a great mirror for fucking, for watching ourselves, but now I would get to watch as I penetrated my ass – and so would Connor. He answered the call right away. 'Show me that sweet body I miss so much,' he said. 'Stand back, that's it,' he coaxed as I positioned myself so my breasts were on display. 'Pinch those pretty nipples for me, and come a little closer so I can make sure you're doing it hard enough.' Just hearing him say that made me wet, and doing it? Well, that had my pussy literally dripping, in a way I knew he'd be able to see once I bent over. 'Good girl. You're almost ready for the clamps. But first I want to see that ass. I want it ready for my cock when you get home from your tropical paradise there.'

I shuddered as I dropped my breasts, turned around and bent over, hoping my ass was in the right position. 'Very good, Farrah, especially since I can see your ass and your pussy from this angle. Now hold your cheeks open for me, the way you do when I run my tongue along your crack.' They were just words, right? But they weren't, not really. From him, they were more than words, and hearing them made me want to hop on a plane home so I could hear them right in my ear. I held myself open and waited while he admired me, his whistle followed by the unmistakable sound of him stroking his cock. 'Touch your hole, baby. Press your finger there and show me you're ready for your present. After you get the plug in you can put on the clamps.'

I automatically followed his instructions, and quickly

## Do Not Disturb

found that the sensation of touching my own anus, knowing Connor was watching my every move, was almost as powerful as when he touched me there. I genuinely wanted more, and, without even asking him, reached for the lube and the plug. I stayed bent over so he could observe my ass as I coated the toy thoroughly, then set the lube bottle on the ground and brought the toy to my ass. I wasn't sure if it would be a challenge to get it in, but to my delight it wasn't at all, especially when I began playing with my clit with my free hand. 'Did I tell you that you could touch yourself, Farrah? No, I didn't,' he asked and answered. 'Just keep going now that you've started, but know that the nipple clamps will have to go on extra tight to teach you a lesson about listening.'

With that, the plug slipped all the way in. I let go and gasped as I tightened my anal muscles around it. It felt wonderful yet strange. I'd never used a plug on myself, and probably wouldn't have on my own. But under Connor's tutelage I felt exposed, like the whole world was watching and knew what a slutty girl I was, one who couldn't go another minute without something filling her ass. 'That's right. Now I want you to twist it around, the way I would if I were there.' I did, slowly, feeling each sensation as the toy penetrated me. 'It's too bad I'm not there to hold your cheeks open.' The more he talked, the more aroused I got; I wasn't sure if I'd have been able to do this in front of Connor, with him observing me from inches away. But from a whole country away? That was OK, and in a way felt even more intimate. Before Connor, there'd been times in my life when I'd tumbled into bed with someone I'd just met, but what we were doing now required a level of trust that only came from knowing each other so deeply for so long. He knew how far he could push me, and I knew that he'd be there to take care of me, even if 'there' was a virtual place. The more I twisted the toy, the more I knew I needed something in my pussy, too. I didn't care what, as long as it filled all the places that were now aching and empty.

'How does it feel, Farrah?' he asked when I dropped my hand and looked behind me at him. Seeing him with his hard cock resting in his hand, I whimpered, wishing I could wrap my lips around the head and lick him slowly, savouring the drop of pre-come I could see. I shuddered and shifted so I was on my knees, the plug still carefully snug between my cheeks. Connor slapped his hands together, the sound startling against the quiet.

'Tell me, right now, or you're going to have to spank that pretty ass until it's bright red.'

'It feels good. But it makes me want your cock inside me.' That wasn't a lie, but it wasn't the full truth, either. I wanted his cock, for sure, but I liked the distance, or, at least, how we were using it. I felt even more wanton than usual, which made me shove three fingers inside myself. It wasn't my usual way of masturbating, but in the moment it felt perfectly right – not a substitute for my husband, but a complement.

'That's good, baby, that's what I want to see. Get yourself nice and wet, and then you're going to put those clamps on.' I trembled as he said that, my fingers sleek and slippery as I realized how fully under his spell I was, and how much I liked it. 'Now take out those fingers and wash your hands and we're going to have some fun with your nipples. I want to make sure they're nice and sore and sensitive so you don't forget about me out there in paradise.'

I didn't tell him I could never forget about him, sore nipples or not. I eased my fingers out, my pussy contracting at the loss of penetration. I stood, but the minute I started to walk away, staying in view of the laptop for as long as possible, I realised that walking while wearing a butt plug between my cheeks was very different from not wearing one. Every step produced a twinge of arousal, a reminder that I was doing far more than placing one foot in front of the other. By the time I got to the bathroom, I ached to touch myself again. Instead, I rinsed my fingers and stared at my reflection, my cheeks pink, my breasts heavy with desire.

I walked back towards the vision of Connor's dick in his hand, my naked body in a smaller picture on the screen, envisioning myself wearing the plug while out with

Connor sometime. I pulled out the clamps and dangled them for him to see. 'Oh, I know what they look like, sweetheart. Now I want to know what they look like on you. I'm going to put those on you when you get home and make you jingle while you fuck me.'

I smiled at him, but when I started to move the lever of one clamp to attach it to my nipple, he stopped me. 'Wait a second, honey. You know I'd warm up those nipples better than that. Take your left nipple into your mouth and suck on it.' He knew I was capable of that because he'd pressed my nipples into my mouth before. I put down the clamp and lifted my nipple to my lips, glancing up to make sure he could see me. I teased myself – and Connor – with a lick, surprised at how powerful that relatively soft wet caress felt as it travelled through me. 'I told you to suck on it, Farrah,' he said. So I did, for a second pretending it belonged to another woman, then sucking hard before placing it between my teeth. I twisted my other nipple, pinching as hard as I thought I could stand, feeling my pussy again straining for release. 'OK, that's good, now I want you to wear those clamps for me.'

I picked one up, excited to feel its fierce heat, but nerves – ones I didn't even realise I had – got the best of me, making me fumble with the clamp. It fell, and Connor said, 'Do I need to call down to the hotel and send someone up there to help you put those on? Because

## Do Not Disturb

I will, Farrah, if that's what you need to appreciate my gift.' I trembled as I listened and tried again, this time placing my hard nub between the rubber-tipped ends of the clamp, then sliding the lever up and up.

'Aahh,' I moaned when it started to hurt, but Connor insisted I clamp it a little higher.

'That looks just about right,' he said when I angled my breast towards the camera. I had an easier time with the second clamp, though the combined heat of both clamps sent waves of sweet pain through my body. 'Jingle them for me, like my own personal Christmas present,' Connor instructed, and I wiggled my shoulders and chest, then lightly flicked the bells. 'You must be very wet by now. I want to see you put something inside your pussy. Get out that vibrator – I want to see you come using it. Lie on the bed, and put the laptop next to you.' I climbed onto the bed and made sure Connor could see me, put the batteries in the toy, then got on my hands and knees so the butt plug wouldn't press into me at the wrong angle. I'm used to being on my back when I use my vibrator, but what I was used to had flown out the window when I first started Skyping with Connor.

I pressed the thick head of the toy against my slit, then pushed backwards and pressed it inside me. Once it was in about halfway, I turned it on, the rabbit going to work on my clit. I eased the toy deeper inside me until it was as deep as it could get, and started to rock back and forth while the bells danced beneath me. I knew Connor was stroking his cock, but I couldn't see or hear much above the whirring of the toy and my own heavy breathing.

I shut my eyes and squeezed my ass and pussy, and was instantly rewarded, the sensations compounded the more I focused on my pleasure. I'd done my part in following Connor's commands; now I was reaping the benefits, and the toys were my new lovers, there to please me and only me. I bucked back and forth with abandon, crying out as I came closer and closer to orgasm, the vibrator almost slipping from my grasp as I got wetter and wetter. Finally, I slammed it deep inside me, the force and the continued dual vibrations of the toy making me grit my teeth lest I scream so loud I alerted security. It took me at least a minute to relax enough to turn the vibrator off and ease it out. I slowly sat up, back on my knees, still aware of the light plug between my asscheeks, the silver bells dangling from my nipples.

Connor wore a look of pure joy on his face. 'That was amazing, Farrah. *You* are amazing.' I smiled, a tear falling down my cheek. How much I'd have given for him to take me in his arms just then. 'I'm here and ready for you to take off those clamps and remove the plug. Take a deep breath, baby.' I smiled at him briefly, then looked down, trying to prepare for the denouement of my sex-toy adventure. I guided my fingers into place and then quickly eased down the lever of first one clamp, then the other.

*Do Not Disturb*

I bit my lip as the blood rushed back into my nubs, and cradled my breasts in my palms. Then I reached behind me and eased the plug out. My body still felt full from where all three toys had worked their magic.

'Next time you get a trip offer, I'm coming with you, Farrah. No question about it. Maybe we can put on a show of our own for someone else like this. Same time tomorrow?' he asked.

I nodded. 'Of course. I'll flash you any time you want.'

\* \* \*

When I made it down to the lobby the next morning, after sleeping soundly and dreaming of Connor using my toys on me, I found a package waiting for me. On the box it said, 'From Connor. USE ONLY WITH ME.' I was curious, but if I'd learned anything from the first package, it's that Connor knows what he's doing, and is the best gift-giver I could ask for.

## *Suite Surrender*
## *Willow Sears*

I'm feeling decidedly slutty so I'm resolved to give Seth what he's been wanting all this time. Hopefully it will be the most memorable birthday present he has ever had. It will certainly be one hell of a surprise when I turn up at the hotel out of the blue to deliver his kinky treat. It was the four-poster that instilled the thought. Once I'd found out he'd bagged himself one of the posh establishment's feature suites, the seed of an idea began to form within. And since I am secretly such a dirty girl, anything that provokes me to use words like 'seed' and 'within' in the same sentence whilst he is on my mind simply has to be pursued.

Seth is many women's idea of the perfect man and there were a lot of jealous faces at the wedding. He is handsome and fit. He is charming, open and very sexy. He works hard and brings home the bacon. He gives

## Do Not Disturb

a lot and asks for little in return, which is why it bugs me so much to have him deprived in the bedroom. I have plenty of sleepless nights mulling over him and his particular kink. I've opened bottles of wine and had Carla and sometimes even a couple of my other friends round to discuss the issue. However, the fact still remains that due to certain apparently insurmountable reservations, poor, lovely Seth quite rightly feels himself doomed to go through life without having his naughty fantasy come true. It made my heart bleed to think I couldn't act to change it. My one immediate aim should be to somehow make it happen for him. Then I heard about this hotel trip and all my ideas suddenly crystallised.

I'm amazed the thought hadn't come to me sooner, although this instance does seem unique in its potential. He goes away often to present on courses, although usually further afield. Here he is a mere twenty miles away in deepest Oxfordshire, leaving him well in range of a swoop by Yours Truly. Any visit must be of a hit-and-run nature because wives and girlfriends are never allowed to tag along. Normally only a single room would be booked, but it seems his colleagues are keenly aware they have made him cancel his day off and his birthday plans at very short notice, just to shore up their shortfall on this course. Added to that, he must undertake the bulk of the work, including the morning presentation on Day Two, straight after breakfast, which would mean a cripplingly early start if he was to travel from home, despite its closeness to the hotel. The plush room is thus compensation for spoiling his birthday, and since they are making this effort it's only fair that I also do my bit.

The short notice has stopped me dwelling upon the gravity of my plan. Better to just leap right in without thought. The longer I don't act the harder it will become. Everything seems to fit so why not just go for it? The preparation is minimal. I've ascertained what time he and his colleagues are having dinner in the hotel restaurant, so I know when to make my unseen arrival. The bedposts have been provided so really it's just a question of finding something to secure the wrists with. Seth also likes the idea of using a blindfold. I'm sure a sleep mask would do the job and since the hotel's website says they provide such things in their suites he should be in luck. He likes the idea of a gag too, but that's not something I'm going to have lying about the house so he will have to do without. I know this is supposed to be about him but I also need to consider my part in proceedings. I mean, it is a really, *really* big thing I'm going to do. I need to ensure it goes the way I see it in my head. I'm sure he will realise it is better like this.

The toughest part will be securing entry to his room without his knowledge, so that I am already in place on the bed on his return. I will need a room key, and the receptionist might not want to do that without checking

## Do Not Disturb

with him first. It is too risky to just turn up and hope, so I decide to ring first. The female receptionist sounds approachable, so I give her the whole blah-di-blah backstory on Seth: how I am his wife of a month; how his work is going to make me miss this, his first birthday with us as a married couple; how this date is also something of an anniversary for us since we met five years ago on this very day at his party; how I'd love to sneak into his room to give him a surprise gift of my own.

I try not to make it sound dirty. I don't mention the black net stockings I will be bringing in my bag to be used as wrist restraints. I don't fill her in on Seth's longtime bondage fantasies and why I have suddenly decided that this is the perfect time to do something about them. I will let her draw her own conclusions about what my 'gift' is to be. Seth must have checked in by now so she will have already seen what kind of a dreamboat he is and why I cannot bear to pass up this opportunity. Hopefully she will not let jealousy stand in the way. She tells me she will have to clear it with the manager first. I tell her to do so, and that I will be along before eight that evening, hoping this will present them with a *fait accompli.*

Frankly they should let me in because it is a waste of a room otherwise. I see from the pictures that the hotel is a beautiful Tudor manor house in red brick and black timbers. The front is wisteria-clad. The lawns are immaculate and surrounded by box hedging, and there is a walled herb garden too. The rooms are sumptuously appointed and sympathetic to the age of the building, hence the four-posters in the feature suites. However, let's be honest, four-posters are Sex Beds. They call his room the Wolsey Suite but they might as well have called it the Bondage Bedroom. Such beds are a kind of jokey hint that we stiff-upper-lipped Brits aren't averse to saucy antics after all. Never in the history of hotel-room booking has a four-poster suite been reserved without some accompanying nudge-nudge, wink-winkery. It's almost the law. So, having seen that Seth has been booked singly into such a room, they should be glad I plan to turn up to make the best use of it.

Somehow I manage to keep my legs crossed all afternoon, a feat I normally find nigh-on impossible. The nerves bite as the hour draws near. For the first time I begin to think of how it might backfire. However, my naughty side won't be denied, and it drives me on. I go over my stuff. There are things to be secreted that I don't want spilling out of my handbag at reception as I search for my purse. I have the genius idea of wrapping them as presents. I still have the boxes they came in so no one will be able to guess what is concealed beneath the gift wrap.

I also decide to wear the stockings rather than hide them in my bag as originally planned. The evenings are

## Do Not Disturb

just about cool enough for hosiery and I think I can avoid looking too much like a tart. I settle on wearing black: a simple blouse and a knee-length skirt. I have to wear heels, of course, but I've dispensed with any kind of cleavage display, to keep the look sophisticated rather than flirty. It's my bottom he most lusts after anyway, not my breasts. From behind her desk the receptionist might think Seth has somehow got himself hitched to a consummate prude, and let's face it, she would be right.

I check my watch yet again and do the calculations. I want to be there in good time. Suddenly it's crept up on me and I realise I must go. I take a deep breath, check my handbag again, ask myself for the umpteenth time if I'm sure I know what I'm getting myself into, then get in the car and drive before I lose my nerve. The journey is easy and I know exactly where I am going. I am impelled there through anticipation despite the growing butterflies. I must be bold or things will fall down. I pull into the hotel driveway at 7.15. If I am right he will still be in his room, so it is time to bring Phase One into operation.

I park up and breeze into reception. The girl there turns out to be the one I spoke to earlier. She also turns out to be much better looking than she sounded on the phone. With me in this mood I can't help but eye her up even if I am trying hard not to appear like a hussy. I think she notices but I'm not sure the manager arrived in time to catch me gawping at her backside as she bent to find me a form. I try to keep up my deception as the good wife, there merely to deliver a surprise gift, rather than being there to provide the Birthday Boy with the kind of kinky sex he has been hankering after for so long.

The manager's smiles mask his suspicion. He doubtless suspects a scam, in which I gain access to my supposed husband's bedroom without his knowledge only to fleece the room and disappear back into the night. He wants me to fill out a form, which I am OK with. He also wants me to leave a credit card. I agree, but point out that although it is current, it is still printed with my maiden name, me not being organised enough yet to have changed my details. He studies the card, the suspicions starting to strengthen. I say I am happy for him to take my picture on his phone for added security. I then tell him I want a table for dinner at eight and to pay now for a bottle of champagne to be delivered to the suite at nine. This convinces him I am neither thief nor con-artist, and thus I get my very own key to the Wolsey Suite. With this victory sealed I sweep out of the hotel again and go and sit in my car for a while to catch my breath and bask in the smugness of my success.

I am just about on schedule. I look at my phone, studying the text message I have typed in readiness. The wording didn't take long to compose. It was the first thing that came to me and I think it sums up my thoughts very succinctly. It says, very simply:

## Do Not Disturb

*I want us to fuck tonight.*

I press the button to send it and my belly flips because it has begun. I can almost see the fragments of the message flitting through the ether into the grand hotel entrance and up the stairs to his room. I hope he is naked when he receives it, still wet from the shower. I hope his prick springs up as he reads what I've written. I hope he gasps and has to grab his stiff cock from the jolt of excitement my words bring. The urge to masturbate sweeps over me again, fuelled by a combination of excitement and nervousness at my reckless action. I practically have to sit on my hands to prevent me tugging up my skirt right there in the hotel carpark. I told myself before to keep calm at this point. A reply won't be immediate if he is still in the shower or dressing. He most certainly is not used to getting such messages from me, so it will come as a bolt from the blue, one he will no doubt need time to consider. Still, when five minutes have crept by with no response, my jitters worsen. Maybe it was just too rude, too unexpected. Maybe he thinks it is a prank. Perhaps for some reason he can't read it – it would be just my luck to have picked the one day he left his phone at home, or had the battery run flat.

I jump when my phone beeps to show a message received. My hands are shaking. I rush to read his reply, hoping he will stick to the script I have played out in my head. His message is pretty much as I thought it would be. It says:

*!!!What???*

I smile because I can picture his surprise and because I already know what to say next. I type quickly and send my reply:

*I want to give you a birthday present you will never forget. I want to come all over your cock.*

He is too cool and too self-assured to mince his words. My message will shock him but I have nailed my colours to the mast and I am sure he will do the same. I am correct. His reply comes back quickly:

*We both know that can't happen.*

Little does he know it both can and will. This conversation is going almost exactly as I had played it out in my head, so I know my next line:

*It can, even if someone has to be tied to the headboard to make it happen.*

That's the killer line, the one to slay him. I guess it stunned him into silence because there is a little while before I get his answer:

*It's a lovely thought, but ...*

But nothing, Seth.

I leave him hanging with all this in mind, not wanting to spring the surprise too quickly. My breath is coming in heaves and I have to concentrate to bring it under control. That last text of mine will have struck right at his heart. I picture him standing, staring at his phone and wondering what to make of my messages. I imagine his beautiful cock hard from the thoughts I have given him, him there naked with his prick stretching out, swollen with rude ideas. I can see him clearly in my mind's eye and that gets me back on top of things. He will be rushing now, aware that he will be late down for dinner. He might have to squeeze his still thickened fat prick into his tight cotton boxers. His head will be a jumble, that one word 'tied' inducing all sorts of images. I bet he thought he would never have such promises made to him, least of all by me.

At 7.50 I am ready to sneak back into the hotel. I go to the bar area to await my table. From my vantage point I can see through a glazed partition into the dining room. His group are there, already into their starters. I see him and my heart leaps. He is looking wonderful in a lilac shirt, open at the neck. He scrubs up very well in smarter clothes. It is odd to watch him candidly, knowing he cannot see me. His cheeks are a little flushed and I know it's a hangover from the excitement of my texts. I bet he is dying for my next one to arrive, hoping that I will keep up with the flirtation, even if it makes his crotch bulge under the table. Despite the shock I've given him he is just about managing to be his usual charming, humorous self. Being centre stage is natural to him. Some think him a bit brash and selfish but they don't know him well enough. Self-confidence is a gift and he wouldn't be who he was or where he was without it. Too bad that marriage has dampened his adventurous side, but that is all about to change.

I want him, desperately. I almost want him enough to slide from my stool at the bar and march in there to brazenly bare myself for him and tell him to come and get it. I have never been so horny for him and he deserves it. He deserves me in this mood. The waiter tells me my table is ready and I stand slowly and prepare myself for my grand entrance. I wish I'd worn a shorter skirt to show more of my stockings off. I am glad this one at least is tight around my curvy behind. In I go, eyes fixed his way. I know he likes to surreptitiously check out other girls so he won't allow the entrance of any young female to pass him by.

His eyes come to mine and I watch the flicker of appreciation followed by recognition and amazement. His jaw drops open. I know he will be feeling the same shiver that is currently sweeping through me. His belly is probably doing as many cartwheels as my own. He says nothing. He watches as I sit at my table not ten feet from his and calmly study the menu. I told him it was going to happen. Now he might begin to properly believe. Before the waiter has a chance to leave I've ordered a plate of Chicken Something and a glass of white wine. I'm hungry for more, in truth; the nerves have left me famished but I need to be finished and upstairs for when the champagne arrives.

## Do Not Disturb

I don't look at him. I try to put on an air of nonchalance as I compose my next text message:

*Did you ever dream you would have your naughtiest fantasies come true, knowing that your wife was the biggest prude on the planet?*

I run through the sequence of my plan again in my head and then press 'send'. The double beep of his phone, heard above the chatter at his table, tells me that the message has landed. I still don't look up, although I know his head is bowed as he reads it. He cannot reply without drawing attention to himself but I know he is dying to. I can feel his eyes burning into me. I know he wants to be inside me. I feel a swell of power in my belly, which drives away the prior self-consciousness. It feels fabulous to be here now, so close to him yet distant, seducing him without even opening my mouth. I send him another text:

*The stockings I'm wearing will act as the ties.*

His phone beeps and he fumbles beneath the table to read it. I even bring my legs out from under the table and pretend to adjust my shoes, just to give him a better view of my fishnets. I'm sure he wants to vault over and shag me where I sit. Their main meals arrive and their conversations are replaced by noises of appreciation and the clatter of cutlery on china. I compose another text, knowing he is watching me, this one designed to leave him in no doubt about my slutty boldness. It reads:

*An Erotica Collection*

*I'm not going home tonight until I have fucked the arse off you.*

That one has to make his cock stiff, even if all the others have not. He loves my smutty side. My food arrives too and I dig in, glad it gives me something other than him to focus on. The chicken is delicious and the wine well needed. I'm feeling far more relaxed now, my stomach calm enough to accept the food. I'm sat here all alone but I feel fine. I'm surrounded by oak-panelled sumptuousness, eating excellent food, and I don't feel ridiculous. I'm feeling like I'm starring in my own private period drama. God, I love hotels like this one – there is just something so *naughty* about them, like they are specifically designed for trysts and improper liaisons.

Think about it – after you have been spoiled by all the grandeur, once you are in your room that's all it is: a room with a bed in it. What else is there to do but use the bed? There will be a bathroom, usually smarter than the one you have at home, kitted out with expensive soaps and hand creams. The bath always looks big enough for two and you can run it as deep as you like. Everything is there to prepare you for a long night of passion. Champagne can be had without need of a shop or a fridge to chill it. In the morning dropped towels and unmade beds will be seen to by an invisible maid. All your secrets will be cleansed by ones who know only of discretion. All seems sumptuous and thrilling, most

## Do Not Disturb

especially the scintillating thought of having sex in an unfamiliar place, in someone else's bed, knowing that you need not worry about leaving any evidence behind.

You can be whoever you want in such places, sign in with any name, create whatever fiction you desire. It feels more fantasy than reality, and that will help me go through with it without thought of consequences. It seems ridiculous that *anyone* could get so het up about what I plan to do with him tonight. It's only a couple of wrist restraints, that's all – just a bit of trust in your partner and the acceptance of some adventure. It's merely a couple of knots and maybe a blindfold, nothing more. In these surroundings you would think it perfectly natural. With the bed they have provided it seems stupid not to. It's just a bit of nothing-to-be-alarmed-about, good old-fashioned English bondage. With maybe a bit of bum-sex thrown in, just for good measure.

Their plates are being cleared and I can sense he is itching to talk to me. He surely won't be stupid enough to approach me at my table. I need to be elsewhere, but I don't want him to follow me out. I compose my final text. I bide my time until the waiter comes to take their dessert order and then I send it. The message reads:

*I will be waiting for you.*

I hear the double beep on his phone and watch his furtive efforts to read it. One of his colleagues loudly jokes,

'Is that your new missus, checking up on you?'

There are laughs all round and I snatch a glimpse of him to see his face flush a little. He mumbles the reply,

'Yeah, something like that.'

I get up and leave just as he is about to give his order to the waiter, knowing he cannot follow.

Indeed, 'something like that'. There's the thing, you see: I am not Seth's wife. That frigid cow Carla is. I might have ended up married to him, if things had gone differently. We both met him on the same night, at that party for his birthday five years ago today. I fancied the pants off him then and told him so too. Unfortunately I drank a little too much and got waylaid and ended up in some cupboard with Andrew Bloody Mathis. Carla ended up with Seth, and they have been together since. OK, they are a good couple, in most respects. He and I would have been a much better couple. It is easy to pretend to be his wife because it is a fiction I often play out in my head. I have always flirted with him but never once pushed it – even though I know things could definitely happen between us – all because she is my friend.

But she keeps coming to me moaning about their sex life, about how kinky she thinks he is because he wants to try a bit of bondage. She tells me all in great detail. I get to hear all about Seth, every little thing. I know him intimately, better than he realises, because of the secrets Carla seems compelled to share. I welcome these extra insights into his character, but not the way she puts him down. If she cannot love him for what he is she doesn't deserve him at all.

However much she claims she loves him she still uses the bondage thing against him, like he is somehow failing and betraying her for wanting to try something barely a notch up from vanilla sex, like he is *disgusting* to ask her to indulge him. I simply cannot see it that way. It sounds so fabulously exciting, so gloriously intimate. It drives me spare that she is such a ridiculous prude. I *hate* that having claimed him she now wants to snuff out his passion when there are others who would die for a chance to share in it. I get to spend evenings drinking wine and pulling my hair out as she moans about how perfect he would be if he wasn't such a *perv*. I said to her, little more than a month ago I said it, at her hen night,

'If you can't make him truly happy why are you going to marry him?'

'Because I love him,' she replied, 'and I'm hoping he will change.'

He gives her everything and all he asks is this one little thing in return, but she just can't bring herself to do it. Well, I can. She might be my friend but Seth is too, and he is far too downright gorgeous to go to waste like this, to be trapped like this. What she doesn't know won't harm her, but I can't let him suffer in silence when I am longing to make it right.

I enter the Wolsey Suite and flick on the light. There is the bed, not as big as I'd imagined but definitely suited to my purpose. The champagne will be here in ten. I estimate Seth will be another half-hour, holding out for a decent period before making his excuses and leaving the others to drink the night away. I kick off my shoes and sit on the bed to carefully remove my stockings. I tie one, by the end, to each of the posts at the head of the bed, then lay them out upon the crisp white pillows, so they are clearly visible. I go into the bathroom to prepare as best I can before the champagne arrives. The porter brings it at nine sharp, and sits it in an ice bucket near the bed. I don't care that he can see the stockings tied to the posts. Let him think what he likes; he doesn't know me. Let him scuttle off and wank over it for all I care. Hotels are for fucking and that's what I'm here to do.

I pour myself a glass of bubbly, take out the two wrapped parcels from my bag and place them on one of the bedside chests. I then strip off my skirt and blouse and go finish my ablutions. I'm feeling in control. There is only one obstacle to overcome and that is the matter of his wedding vows, so recently uttered. He and I, though, we have always had a special understanding, an agreement that we would both one day make it happen, even if it was supposedly said in jest. I know what to do, just in case he does have any second thoughts. I remove my bra, place a pillow at the very end of the bed and bend

## Do Not Disturb

myself over it, so my body is flat on the mattress whilst my feet stay on the floor and my bottom is pushed up by the pillow. It will be the first thing he sees as he enters. He's not going to be able to say no to that.

On a whim I go for broke, reaching down and raising my hips to push my knickers down around my thighs. I should take them off but there is no time. I can hear the fire door opening in the corridor and I know it is him approaching. He is going to get his first view of my bare arse. Let's hope he hasn't brought anyone with him! I must look such a slut with my panties half down. Good. I know he will see my wetness but I don't care – he caused it, after all. I hear the key in the lock and then the sound of the door opening, followed swiftly by him gasping and saying my name in beseeching tones. Well, he can beseech until he's blue in the face – I've told him what I've come for and I'm not leaving without it.

I don't move or look around. The door shuts and I can picture him coming towards me, the bulge at his crotch swelling dramatically, his eyes wide and fixed on my round stuck-out bum. Still without turning I say,

'I don't want kissing, I don't want to fall in love with you. I just want to give you the most memorable night of your life.'

He can't refuse that. I roll onto my back, my bottom now on the edge of the bed and my feet flat on the floor. His saucer eyes travel down my body, down from my breasts to my bare sex. I splay my thighs as far as my constraining knickers allow and give myself a little rub down there because I, unlike his prissy ice-cold wife, am a terribly filthy little slut. I push myself upright and he comes to me. I can see the swell at his crotch, longing to be freed. I undo the buttons at the bottom of his shirt and he quickly sees to the ones at the top, so that in seconds it has been thrown off and his lovely muscular torso is on show.

I go for the belt buckle next and down come his trousers, exposing a pair of tight boxers almost identical to those I'd imagined. The bulge beneath the thin fabric is defined, a thick curl stretching the fabric as it fills. Five years. Five long, frustrating years I've wanted this cock in my mouth. I pull at the band of his boxers and down they come, spilling out his beautiful, warm erection right in front of my face so I can smell it. I watch the rapid final swell now it is free, the bob and pulse from the surge of blood. I see the thin clear stickiness already present at the tip, a sure sign my messages did the trick. I grip the thickness of his meat, my hand looking so small and pale against the darkness of his skin.

He wants me to consume him but I am patient, waiting and absorbing the glory of his prick before hunger finally takes over. I go down on him and he gasps. I bet his wife isn't this fucking slutty. I slurp and suck and take him deep. He grips my hair and stifles his cries. He crams my mouth, making my saliva flow. He feels so slick, so smooth and lovely. I need this cock inside me. I push him onto the bed and struggle with the tangle at his ankles of trousers and underwear and sock and shoes. He shuffles up the bed till his head rests on the pillow, his fingers already caressing the ends of my stockings, tied in readiness for this moment. He smiles at me, knowing that I know.

I climb back onto the bed, coming up at him slowly. In my head I'm like a stalking panther. I use my tongue on his thighs, lapping the skin there, in towards his privates. I run my long nails down his legs as I lick the skin near his genitals. I take his heavy balls into my mouth and give them a quick wet sucking. I lap the length of his shaft along its stretched underside, from balls to tip. I flick the glans rapidly with my tongue, in my mind's eye more snake now than panther. He wants another sucking but I move on, my breasts sliding over his privates as I move up upon him. I lick his belly and his chest, both nipples in turn. Then I am on him, looking down into his eyes, feeling his iron-hard prick pulsing against the length of my wet slit.

He has to bear my weight and he does. I need both hands free. I take the end of one stocking and wrap it around twice, quite tightly, so that his wrist is secure. I fasten it with a single knot. I can feel his chest rising and falling with his heavy breaths beneath me. I give him a little smile and touch my forehead to his, then set about fastening his other wrist. He lies there, always looking into my eyes. I see in his a mix of lust and gratitude. I adjust the stockings in turn, pulling them so that his hands are forced closer to the posts, spreading his arms wide. I reach down and peel off the wet knickers still at my thighs. He is going to get a gag after all. I press the gathering of soggy fabric to his lips and he opens up to take it. I reach for the bedside cabinet and find the sleep mask there. It seems a shame not to let him view it all but this is what he wants, according to frigid Carla.

This is it; this little thing that his wife can't abide but I find so thrilling. She thinks it emasculates him, makes him a sissy. She cannot bear the thought that her big, strong man wants to be tied up and used. She wants it all to go away. She hasn't got the imagination to realise the fantasy. She hasn't got the fire to delight in any power or control over him, but I do. Ever so slowly I mount him, holding his prick beneath me to guide it to my entrance before sinking down upon him centimetre by centimetre. He bites down upon his gag and gasps into it. I ride him, as slowly as my self-control will allow. I am already soaking him, my wetness flowing out onto his balls. It is quite a sacrifice to have the mask and deprive oneself of seeing the bliss on your lover's face, or their bouncing tits. It must be driving him mad not being able to grab my soft arse and squeeze it. It must

*Do Not Disturb*

be driving him mad, this slow, deliberate, teasing pace, when he is dying to slam into me and explode.

This is all he wants, the thing to make his life so infinitely better. This is what his wife cannot bring herself to give him in any form. All he needs is to be tied up by a dirty hussy and used, to be made a bitch by a bitch. He doesn't want to be beaten or spat upon or even have abuse hurled at him. He just wants control taken away from him. He wants to be tormented. So I do. I take him all the way deep and grind against his crotch so that I can take pleasure without driving him close to his own finish. I come off him and tease him with my mouth, flicking my tongue across it then taking him deep. I love the taste of my pussy on his rigid prick.

Whilst using my mouth I push my bottom right out towards his face. I'm feeling so horny I might well have done this even if he didn't have the mask on. I waggle my backside so that the cheeks brush against his face. I know he is dying for me to squash it into him but I won't. I know he can smell my desire and feel the heat from my pussy. I know he would give anything to feast upon me. Having this power over him is incomparably erotic. Why can't his stupid wife see this? He is so strong and forceful, so confident, and yet he has surrendered himself entirely.

I wank him with my hand and with my breasts pressed together against his erection; anything to drive him wild.

Then I sink back down upon him and ready myself for the final onslaught. I build slowly, pushing my hips back and then sliding forward as I rise up on him, like I'm trying to milk every last drop from his balls before I let him explode. Then the pace quickens so my bottom is slapping against his thighs and my pussy against his crotch, spattering him with my juices. I'm telling him how much I love his gorgeous, thick cock and how much I want to suck it and fuck it and feel it up my fat arse.

That is the trigger for him. He bites down hard on the panties in his mouth and wrenches at his restraints, as if to hold me fast while he fires off his spurts inside me. But I won't stop. If he were in control the strength of his climax might check his movement; he wouldn't be able to drive himself on through it. However, he is not in control. He has no way of stopping me wringing every single pulse of electrifying pleasure from his prick and balls. I know that continuing to move upon him will give him a finish of almost unbearable force, but that is what I do. I press down hard on his chest and buck up and down, slapping into him, riding him hard as he tenses and jerks and then sprays my insides with jet after jet of his deliciously hot seed.

When I have drained him dry I climb off. It was a wrenching finish for him but I'm not quite finished. I untie his wrists and remove his mask but leave the gag in place. I don't want him getting all romantic on me now, not before I've shown him his gift. I lie flat on the bed and have him lie on top of me. I can feel his flagging erection wet at my thigh. I rub up against him with my crotch but I know it will need more stimulation than this. He's looking at me like he loves me. I'm sure if that gag came out he would be gabbling all sorts of sweet nothings in my ear. Maybe we would just be kissing. He is upon me and there are some stirrings from below but he is far from being hard enough to fill my saturated puss. I hold his hands and spread my arms, taking them back towards the posts. I suddenly realise it might look like I want to be tied, so I act quickly. I wind the stockings back around his wrists, one at a time. I hold him to me and grind my wet crotch to his, smiling up at him. Then I slide out from underneath him, leaving him face-down flat on the bed. I secure each wrist with a knot in the stocking.

This next treat is one I have devised myself. It doesn't come from Carla's spilled secrets. Instinct tells me that Seth will love it, and I think I understand his naughty side better than anyone. It is not something he would confess to his inhibited wife to wanting but I know he will love me for ever for doing it. I sit at the edge of the bed to unwrap the larger of his gifts. His eyes are already bright with expectation. I'm careful not to let the box give it away before it is open. It falls out onto the bed, a bundle of black vinyl and plastic. I hold it up for him to view properly: a harness fitted with a slender, solid dildo.

There is no trace of shock in his expression but then there is nothing to alarm him here. At six inches it isn't even as long as his own erect prick and it is far less thick, with a very slight upward curve at the tapering tip. If anything it might be a little small, but I know it will enable me to give him a long, slow, delicious fuck that will be etched eternally in his memory. I unwrap the smaller gift, a small bottle of clear lubricant. Still he makes no sound into the gag. He turns his head so his face is at the pillow, awaiting my pleasure.

I don't rush. I keep him flat while I ready him. I patiently work the lubricant in and get him relaxed. When the time comes I draw him up to his knees, his face still in the pillow. He surrenders to me quietly. I fuck him just as I had imagined: slow and deep, driving on so my thighs are flat against his behind and holding there before a gradual outward slide. The joy of doing him like this outweighs even my high expectations. Until you have given a man this pleasure you cannot understand. His prick is hard again within the first minute or so. I take ages so that he can revel in his bliss.

I spread lubricant on my hand and reach below to gently stroke his shaft. Only towards the end do I increase my pace, to push him towards a finish. I undo the harness to leave the dildo inside him, and then slide underneath to take him into my mouth. The slickness on my fingers lets them glide rapidly up and down him as I suck, and

## Do Not Disturb

then he is tensing and gasping into his gag and shooting spurts into my mouth; thinner this time, but no less hot. As he is still shaking and jerking I hear his phone bleep twice. It will be his wife no doubt, the one who selfishly claimed him even though she had no intention of giving him the thing he most wants. That no longer matters one bit, though, because from now on he will always have someone who will.

## *A Touch of Class, a Bit of Rough*
## *Rose de Fer*

The Falkenberg Arms crouched like a giant mythical beast on the cliffs above the Cornish coast. Waves crashed on the rocky beach below and wild countryside sprawled behind it. The stately and sombre façade belied the extravagance of its interior. It was a playground for the fabulously wealthy, an escape from reality. If, that was, the fabulously wealthy could be said to inhabit anything like 'reality'.

That was what Emma thought anyway, as she wore her most subservient smile and said 'sir' and 'madam' and even on occasion 'your Lordship' and 'your Ladyship'. Royalty never checked themselves in, of course; they had people to do that for them.

The ones with real class were lovely. Utterly charming and gracious in the way that only the very well-bred ever were. Like Lord Charnock, the gentleman who had spent the previous summer with them. He had always smiled at Emma and wished her a pleasant afternoon, treating her with as much courtesy as he would any of his peers. It was the *nouveau riche* who put on airs and felt the need to be treated like visiting dignitaries, to constantly remind others – and themselves – that they were at the top of the food chain now.

Emma sized them all up as they registered for their enviably long stays at the Falkenberg Arms. The resort boasted spectacular views of the sea and the surrounding countryside, as well as a luxurious spa and a world-renowned restaurant. On occasion the staff were given little treats from the kitchen – sweets or pastries that weren't good enough for the elite clientele but were still perfectly edible. But that was as far as the generosity of the management went. There were no free passes to the spa or gratis bottles of champagne, no two-for-one meal deals. One of the maids, Kerstin, had even been sacked for eating the chocolates they left on the guests' pillows at night.

'Girl? Are you paying attention? Girl!'

Emma looked up, her face betraying no hint of irritation at the woman who stood tapping her thick beringed fingers on the desk. She was a substantial lady, her breasts straining at the confines of the tailored suit she had no doubt had made to her dream measurements rather than her actual ones. How she must covet Emma's petite figure, her high, firm breasts and tiny waist, her tight little arse, which even now clenched around the rubber shaft of the anal plug Patrick had inserted that morning.

'Yes, madam? How may I help you?'

Emma was the consummate professional, the perfect servant. The guests could flaunt their wealth and power all they wanted and they could do their best to make her feel inferior. But their petty ways never fazed her. In truth, she found some of it almost endearing. She liked to imagine that they were Victorians who'd got caught in some kind of time warp and wound up in a world where people no longer 'knew their place' but had 'ideas above their stations'. They could gape in astonishment at the thought that they couldn't just have a girl whipped because she'd spilled a bit of soot on the carpet whilst blacking the grates. Mmm, now there was a hot fantasy ...

'My husband has booked a suite for us,' the woman said haughtily, as though the information was meant to impress Emma.

'Certainly, madam. What's the name, please?'

'Mountchesney,' she pronounced in a lofty tone, again as though Emma ought to recognise it and be suitably cowed.

Without batting an eye Emma said, 'Ah yes, here it is. Two weeks' stay, is it? I'm sure you'll have a lovely time. If you'll just sign here ...'

*Do Not Disturb*

She offered the woman a pen but she produced her own with a flourish, no doubt afraid of catching whatever 'common' diseases such creatures like Emma must carry.

'Very good, madam. You're in the Penhaligon Suite. Here is your key. I see you've booked dinner every evening with us as well.'

'Yes,' Mrs Mountchesney said, beaming proudly and clearly eager to show off that they could afford to eat £500 dinners every night for two weeks running. 'I'm told the chef trained with Joël Robuchon himself!'

Emma knew that wasn't true but she didn't question the manager's decision to say so on the website. It was just the sort of thing that hooked fish like the Mountchesneys. Emma knew their type: notorious name-droppers who would be boasting to their friends about it for years afterwards.

'I'm sure you'll have a lovely time,' Emma said, her warmth as genuine as a prostitute's orgasm. 'And may I personally welcome you and your husband to the Falkenberg Arms.'

The woman bestowed a false smile of her own on Emma and headed off towards the lift, her meaty backside dogging her like the middle-class background she was clearly so eager to shed.

'What a piece of work!'

Emma turned towards the male voice, maintaining her

sanguine expression until she was sure no one else was around. Then her face broke into a wide grin.

Patrick stood there, lounging in the doorway. His green eyes glittered with mischief as he cupped Emma's bottom, squeezing each cheek to make her gasp.

'How's it feel, naughty girl?' he asked in his lazy Irish drawl.

Emma closed her eyes as her sphincter contracted around the thick shaft of the plug. The sensation reminded her of the previous afternoon, when they'd had anal sex in Major Duckenfield's room while he was out shooting. Patrick had bent Emma over the gold-plated bathtub and fucked her wearing the major's uniform jacket. Its brass buttons and medals had clanged against the porcelain with every thrust, and when they came Emma had watched them both in the huge mirror that took up most of one wall.

The night before that they'd watched the CCTV footage of Lady Hazelride giving Patrick a blowjob in the lift. The chef had lost his bet. Gallic charm notwithstanding, Jean-Michel just didn't have that 'bit of rough' the wealthy older ladies seemed to need so badly, and Patrick had bagged her first.

Emma blushed. 'It feels ... very rude. I love it.'

He laughed softly and nudged his knee up between her legs. 'So what's on the cards for the Mounty-whatsits?'

She sighed at the contact but otherwise gave no sign

that she was anything other than a hotel check-in clerk going about her duties while the room service waiter stood close behind her. She clicked through the screens showing the guests' activities. The Mountchesneys had separate schedules. Naturally, Mrs Mountchesney would be taking full advantage of the spa, submitting her bulk for a relaxing massage – offered by a bevy of Thai girls who pretended they spoke no English – along with the full range of beauty treatments: manicure, pedicure, facial, waxing, aromatherapy. The works. She needed it too. Presumably that was why Mr Mountchesney was off to the golf course and then sailing lessons in the bay.

'Looks like they won't be spending much time in their room,' Emma said, arching an eyebrow at her lover.

'Hmm' was all he said.

Sometimes it was all she could do not to throw herself at him. He was strikingly gorgeous, blessed with looks that would be hot on either a man or a woman. Lean, lanky body, sculpted features, sexy bedroom eyes and a lilting accent that made her weak with desire. He might have been a rake in some gothic romance, the villainous swain who could seduce the good girl away from the bland hero she was meant to wind up with.

'What are they doing tonight?'

Emma smiled. 'Dinner. Of course.'

'Of course. Fancy a date?'

'Oh, I think that could be arranged. I'm off at five.'
'Penhaligon Suite?'
'Mm-hmm.'
'I'll be there.' He gave her bottom another pat and slipped back into the office.

Emma closed her eyes for a moment, savouring the feel of the anal plug. It filled her as his cock had done, stretching her, just painful enough to be bliss.

Dinner would take hours. She would ask Jean-Michel to make sure it did.

\* \* \*

'God, I love this room,' Emma said, tossing her bag onto one of the many plush silk-upholstered chairs.

They might have been in a mediaeval castle, so excessive was the interior design. Rich dark furniture, heavy velvet curtains, unicorn tapestries. No one knew who the hell 'Penhaligon' was but he must have loved his King Arthur stories as a lad. There was even a pair of crossed swords above the fireplace.

'Strip.'

Emma blinked in surprise. 'What, no foreplay?'

'Not yet,' Patrick said. He was the same age she was and had no authority over her, but he was so cocksure she always wound up deferring to him. Not that she would have had it any other way. She often imagined what it would be like if Patrick were in charge of the hotel, the things he could demand of his best front-desk girl, the discipline he could administer when she screwed things up …

'Yes, sir,' she said, giving him a cheeky grin as she began unbuttoning her blouse.

Patrick watched as she turned the act into a little striptease for him, wiggling her bottom as she shimmied out of her skirt, bending right over to unbuckle her Mary Janes and kick them off, raising her legs to slip off her hold-ups.

When she was down to her white lace bra and knickers he placed his hands on her shoulders. Then he turned her around and bent her over so her hands were on the bed. A shiver went through her at the submissive posture and she trembled a little as he peeled her knickers down, exposing her bottom. She was still wearing the plug, of course. She wouldn't have dared remove it without his permission.

'Someone's been a very good girl, I see,' he said, patting her bottom to stimulate the plug inside her. 'But perhaps it's time to take this out. Hold still.'

Emma obeyed as he slowly withdrew the plug, brushing his fingertips along her sex as he slid it out and wrapped it in a tissue. Immediately she wanted it back, wanted to be filled again. With the plug or his cock, she didn't care which. A little shudder went through her and Patrick laughed softly.

'Don't worry, Em. We've got hours yet.' He unhooked

her bra and tossed it aside, then filled his hands with her breasts and pulled her back against him. She sighed as she felt the bulge in his trousers pressing against her.

She had always wanted to fuck in the Penhaligon Suite. She imagined Patrick using one of the swords to cut her dress away, slashing her knickers and pressing the cold blade up against her warm, willing sex. The icy shock of it would only make her hotter. She smiled at the thought of replacing it above the fireplace, stained with her juices.

Patrick turned her around and stepped back to look at her. She chewed her lip as she watched his cock swell even more, threatening to burst free of his tight black trousers. It had taken some time for her to be able to accommodate him in her arse and she loved the way it filled her so completely. She couldn't help but think of all the ladies – and gentlemen, Patrick wasn't fussy – who ordered room service late at night merely to have Patrick bring it up to their rooms. Emma wondered if they also quailed with nervous anticipation at the size of his cock. They certainly tipped him well enough for his 'special services'.

Emma sank back on the bed but Patrick moved away, towards the wardrobe. He opened it and began rummaging inside.

'What are you doing?'

'You're so impatient,' he admonished. He pulled

## Do Not Disturb

something off a hanger with a clatter. 'I said we've got hours.' He tipped her a lascivious wink and moved into the antechamber.

Emma listened to the rustle of fabric and tried to imagine what he was up to. When he appeared again her eyes widened for a moment and then she burst into gales of laughter. He was wearing a voluminous dress in piggy-pink taffeta. The sight was so outrageous and brazen it was sexy. The dress was large enough for both of them and he had to hold it up to keep it from falling down. The curly dark hair peeking out of the plunging sweetheart neckline was the perfect touch.

'I wonder where she was planning on wearing this?' he said.

Emma grabbed her phone out of her bag and Patrick posed and pouted like a supermodel while she snapped several pictures of him.

'Shall I send one to Jean-Michel?' she asked.

'Go on,' Patrick said, beaming proudly. 'He'll never be able to top it.'

She called up the chef's number and sent a picture of Patrick clutching his nonexistent bosom and making a hideous kissy face at the camera. A few seconds later the phone bleeped with an incoming text.

'What's he say?' Patrick asked, still preening in front of the mirror.

'He says it's my turn. Fair enough!' She tossed the

phone on the bed and scurried over to the wardrobe to see what she could find to match.

Mr Mountchesney was considerably smaller than his wife and Emma climbed into his dinner suit with little difficulty. Once Patrick had helped her with the clip-on bow tie they stood side by side admiring the bizarre couple they made in the mirror. Emma sent Jean-Michel another pic and he texted back that he couldn't hope to compete.

'That sounds like we've won,' Patrick said, 'whatever the latest bet was.'

Emma didn't even care. They'd had one kind of fun and now it was time for the other. She stood behind Patrick and reached her arms around his front, to clutch at the bodice of the dress.

Patrick responded in kind, thrusting his hand up between her legs to grip her crotch tightly. The touch sent a jolt of desire through her and she squeezed her thighs around his hand with a sigh.

Patrick's cock stood out like a baton beneath the dress, a ludicrous and strangely erotic sight. Emma sank to her knees and crept underneath the tent of pink taffeta. She wrapped her hand around his cock and slid it gently up and down. She heard him moan and his legs trembled a little. Closing her fingers around his shaft, she squeezed hard, pressing her thumb just underneath the head. He dropped the dress and it fell like a curtain, pooling on the floor around them.

## Do Not Disturb

He lifted her off her feet and carried her to the bed. Then he set about peeling her out of the dinner suit. He flung the jacket aside and by the time he yanked her trousers down she had unfastened most of the buttons of the shirt. He didn't even let her finish stripping; he just pushed her down on the silky counterpane and buried his face in her chest. Emma gasped and threw her hands up to grip the nearest bedpost as he pushed her breasts together, kneaded them roughly and kissed her nipples, sucking and biting.

She rolled her hips, pressing up against him as he rubbed his cock against her sex, teasing her clit with its swollen head but not entering her. He climbed on top, straddling her waist for a moment before moving up to her head. He lowered his cock to her face and she opened her mouth, taking it in greedily. Then he fucked her face, sliding his length in and out with slow languid thrusts.

Emma slowed his rhythm even more so she could catch her breath. She fluttered her tongue around the head and up and down the shaft, enjoying each little twitch and throb. The hot salty taste of his cock made her hungry to feel it elsewhere. Her pussy pulsed with need.

'Please fuck me,' she said in a breathless whisper.

The bed bounced as he clambered off and Emma heard the sharp rip as Patrick tore open a condom. She caught the scent of latex as he returned to the bed and then he surprised her by flipping her over onto her stomach. Then he shoved a pillow underneath her and she shuddered with submissive pleasure as it raised her bottom up, presenting it for him.

'I'm going to fuck that tight little arse,' he said, his voice low and husky with desire. He ran a hand over her cheeks and she trembled. 'But first I want to feel that hot wet pussy.'

Emma whimpered a meaningless response and he slapped her arse smartly, making her yelp.

'I didn't hear you, Em.'

'Yes, please,' she gasped. 'Please fuck my hot wet pussy.'

'And then?'

Her insides swam with delicious shame at being made to say the words. 'And then fuck my tight little arse.'

'That's better.'

He urged her legs wide apart and she braced herself as he pressed the head of his cock against her sex. Then he slid it in with one brutal thrust. She cried out, clutching the counterpane as he began to fuck her, filling her completely with each thrust. Her cries became louder as he gripped her pelvic bones like handles and drove himself in and out, in and out, sending jolts of ecstasy through her sex, her legs, her entire body. He found a steady rhythm, pounding her ruthlessly while she surrendered to the violent passion they had found between them.

'Someday I'm going to tie you down spread-eagled over a table in the kitchen with Jean-Michel,' he said, his words punctuated by powerful thrusts. 'We'll take turns licking honey off your nipples and then he can have your pussy while I fuck your arse.'

'Oh, God, yes,' Emma gasped, imagining the scene.

'Or maybe I'll take you out to the stable block,' he continued. 'Truss you up with leather straps and halters and an iron bit in your mouth to stop you from screaming. Then I'll whip that little arse with a riding crop. Ride you till you drop.'

Her face blazed with the delirious mix of shame and desire. He could do anything to her, anything at all, and she'd surrender and love every minute of it.

When he began slowing his strokes she knew what was coming next. She wanted it, even craved it, but it still embarrassed her. She imagined it was how all those lonely ladies felt who bought Patrick's services late at night. Conditioned to believe that rough, nasty sex was something 'ladies' didn't want. Or shouldn't want.

Emma had the same neurotic programming and overcoming it again and again was part of the thrill. She loved being made to beg for the rudest favours, to display and debase herself in lewd ways that left her head swimming with filthy lust. His sadistic fantasies had whipped her into a frenzy.

'I want your hard cock in my arse,' she panted, her legs trembling with the effort of staying spread so widely, at making such an exhibition of herself.

Patrick drew his finger up between her cheeks, making

her shudder. Then he fisted a hand in her hair and pulled her head back roughly, forcing her back to arch, urging her bottom up even higher.

'Maybe one of your posh gentlemen will order you for room service sometime,' he said. 'I'll deliver you to him on a silver tray and he can play with you all night.'

Emma thought she would faint.

When he finally took her she nearly came. She felt the powerful twinges in her sex as he fucked her arse and each slow deliberate thrust made her want to scream from the intoxicating blend of pleasure and pain. Emma clenched herself around his cock, writhing beneath him. He obliged her mute entreaty with a series of sharp swats to her bottom. He let go of her hair and she buried her face in the bed, slipping one hand underneath herself to touch her clit. She slid her fingers back and forth across it as Patrick continued to fuck her, calling her a dirty little slut, his dirty little slut.

Her pussy tingled with the rising throbs of a powerful climax and then she came so hard it made her ears ring. Patrick came too, his cock spasming violently inside her arse, intensifying and prolonging her own orgasm.

It took her some time to drift back down to reality. She heard the rustle of taffeta as Patrick presumably replaced the clothes in the wardrobe. She got shakily to her feet and smoothed out the bed and pillows, then tried to get dressed. Her hands were trembling so much

## Do Not Disturb

she couldn't fasten her bra and Patrick smiled indulgently as he helped dress her. How he was able to manage it she didn't know.

\* \* \*

Emma was sore for days, the kind of soreness she loved. It made her job both challenging and delightful as she smiled serenely at the guests and told them to enjoy their stay. But after a while she began to get restless. She wanted more.

Then one afternoon she got a text from Patrick. Trade places with Oksana, it said. Emma stared at the message in confusion. Oksana was one of the maids, a pretty Russian girl she knew Patrick had his eye on. Emma had been watching her too. There was something in the girl's impish smile that said she'd be up for some of their games.

Before she could reply her phone bleeped again. And clothes.

Emma blushed as she tucked her phone away and waited. Oksana arrived a few minutes later, her eyes dancing with mischief as she took Emma by the hand and led her into the office. She closed the door and undressed without a word, holding out her uniform for Emma with an expectant look.

Emma obeyed the wordless command and took off her smart skirt and blouse. Then Oksana helped her into the maid's uniform, adjusted her white lace pinafore and tied it in a large bow at the back. She smoothed the short flirty skirt down over Emma's bottom, lingering for a teasing moment before nodding her approval.

'You go now,' she said. 'Trevenan Suite. I think you are in trouble.'

'Trouble?'

But Oksana didn't reply; she merely smiled as she took Emma's place behind the reception desk.

Emma pressed the button in the lift with trembling fingers and took deep breaths to calm her fluttering heart. She couldn't imagine what Patrick had arranged but the maid's uniform made her feel both submissive and vulnerable, like a schoolgirl at the mercy of someone else's authority.

When she reached the Trevenan Suite she raised her hand and gave a tentative little knock. A voice told her to enter – a deep and cultured English voice that clearly wasn't Patrick's. She thought she recognised it and as she stepped meekly inside she gasped. Lord Charnock stood there, frowning slightly at her.

She opened her mouth to stammer out an apology, although she didn't know what she was meant to be apologising for.

'Well, stand up straight, girl,' he told her sharply.

She obeyed instantly, her legs shaking, her face burning. The crisp authoritarian tone was so different from the kind and gentle voice he'd spoken to her with last summer and it immediately sent hot wet pulses through her sex.

Lord Charnock crossed the room to stand directly in front of her, gazing sternly at her and forcing her to meet his eyes. He drew his finger slowly along the surface of a polished mahogany table and held it up for her to see the dust.

'Does that look clean to you, girl?'

Emma swallowed and shook her head, her sex pounding with arousal. 'No, sir,' she murmured. 'I'm sorry, sir.'

'No, you're not,' Lord Charnock said, and Emma caught the hint of a smile in his expression. He seated himself on the ottoman at the foot of the bed and rolled up his right sleeve. Then he patted his knee. 'But you will be.'

## *An Airport, Anywhere*
## *Elizabeth Coldwell*

Nowhere is as lonely as the lobby of an airport hotel at two in the morning. The guests are all safely in their rooms, long past the need for room service; the bar is closed and no one is waiting to check in, or out. Sitting at the front desk, watching the minutes tick slowly by and wondering if she'll have anything of any significance to do before the night ends, Lauren feels like the last remaining woman on Earth.

This could be an airport anywhere. Stepping out of the blandly decorated lobby, a curious traveller could hail a taxi and be whisked to downtown Tokyo, or Los Angeles, or Nairobi. Nothing distinguishes it from any other hotel in the parent company's extensive chain, all priding themselves on the same high level of service that insists on having a receptionist to staff the desk twenty-four hours a day, whether one is needed or not.

## *Do Not Disturb*

When Lauren leaves at the end of her shift, it will be to catch the Tube, making the short journey through the grey dawn of West London to her flat in Boston Manor. Sometimes she wishes she was somewhere more exotic, somewhere where the air smells of frangipani rather than exhaust fumes and the planes take off over a rolling blue ocean, but mostly she's happy in her job. The long hours of quiet give her time to work on her writing, scribbling longhand in the jotter that she takes with her everywhere. She pens urban fantasy, tales of a demon hunter called Liliana, who strides through a city that's almost but not quite New York, dispatching monsters and having impossibly wild, kinky sex with her half-vampire lover, Brogan. None of these stories has been published as yet, but she's sure it's only a matter of time before someone recognises her talents.

Though they'll never know it, half the characters in her books are inspired by people who work in the hotel, or the rare guest who stands out enough from the crowd to imprint themselves on her memory. The grumpy demon that Liliana pushes to his death, impaling him on a cathedral gargoyle, is based on the man who complained about everything from the thread count of his sheets to the lack of hazelnuts in his breakfast muesli. Nothing less than polite to his face, Lauren has used her real feelings about his overly pernickety behaviour to consign him to a gruesome fictional fate.

When it comes to the many and varied sex scenes in her stories, the guests have played their part in their creation, too. A cute guy checking in may find himself the unwitting inspiration for one of Brandon's buff, well-hung vampire cohorts, or a renegade soldier battling against the evil that corrupts the city. And not everyone will be asleep right now, she knows; human nature being what it is, someone is bound to be fucking in one of the rooms above her head, taking advantage of the thrill that comes from being in strange surroundings with no one to recognise them. Though she's never actually walked in on anyone in action, more than one of the maids has interrupted a couple who forgot, accidentally or otherwise, to leave out the 'Do Not Disturb' sign. The anecdotes involving those who've been caught in the act have been repeated over and over, maybe gaining a little embellishment as they've passed into scandalous legend: the woman handcuffed to the bed in Room 412 while her husband licked chocolate body paint from her naked, restrained body; the black couple watching themselves in the dressing-table mirror as he ploughed his cock in and out of her plump, yielding arse while she crooned, 'Yeah, fuck that booty!'; the respectable-seeming middle-aged gent found masturbating into a white silk stocking, a ball-gag securely stoppering his mouth ...

With so many wicked thoughts running through her head, so many delicious combinations of breasts and mouths, fingers and tongues, cocks and cunts, Lauren soon finds herself on a roll. The words are flowing and she's determined to complete a couple of thousand words before she comes off shift, so it's a while before she notices the red light blinking on the telephone switchboard. When she first got the job, she used to watch for it all the time, anxious to help out whoever wished to speak to her, but those requests were so rare she soon fell out of the habit. Eventually, the sight registers with her. Snatching up the receiver, Lauren hopes she hasn't left the guest waiting too long for a reply. Even in the dead hours of night, when no one expects instant service, it doesn't do to look unprofessional. Whoever's on the other end of that phone might decide to slate her on one of those tourist advisor websites when their trip is over.

'Front desk, Lauren speaking. How may I help you?'

'Hi, Lauren.' The voice is Australian-accented, husky, as though it's been desiccated by the dry air of a long-haul flight. 'This is Greg Jackson, Room 324. The hairdryer in my room doesn't appear to be working. I wondered if you could send someone up to take a look at it.'

Who washes their hair at two in the morning? Lauren can't help but wonder. Smoothly, she assures him, 'I can do better than that, Mr Jackson. I'll have a new hairdryer brought up to you right away.'

It's a wrench to tear herself away from her writing. Liliana and Brogan are in bed together, Liliana keen to show her gratitude to him for saving her from one of the vicious alligator shifters who infest the city's network of sewers. Her skilful tongue is about to tease the sweetest of orgasms from his willingly bound body, mouth engulfing the full length of his straining cock. Lauren loves to write about oral sex almost as much as she loves giving and receiving it, and describing the lovers in their passion has got her all hot and bothered. But Mr Jackson needs his hairdryer, and he needs it now.

Slipping away from the desk, she takes the stairs down a level to where the supply cupboard is located. She unlocks the door with the master key she never allows to leave her side, flips on the light switch and steps inside, to be confronted by shelf upon shelf of plastic-packaged shower caps, miniature bottles of shampoo and shower gel, and packets of individually wrapped shortbread fingers. All the little goodies that help to make a hotel stay more pleasant and, more often than not, depart in the guests' luggage at the same time as they do.

Opposite those are the electrical appliances she's looking for: miniature kettles, big enough to produce enough boiling water for two dainty cups of tea, and beneath those, a box of deceptively small but high-powered hairdryers. Lauren takes one, signs for it in the log. When George, the maintenance man, arrives tomorrow morning, he can take a look at the malfunctioning dryer from Jackson's room, and make an assessment as to whether it can be fixed. Lauren's DIY skills extend as far as changing a plug. Anything else she'll leave to the experts.

She locks up, leaving the room in darkness once more. The lift takes her to the third floor, a soulless Muzak rendition of 'The Greatest Love of All' the soundtrack to her journey. Checking her reflection in the mirrored wall, she smiles in approval. Her dark hair is sleek in its ponytail, her make-up as fresh as when she applied it before starting her shift. She looks professional, capable, willing to help. Stepping out into the hallway, Lauren breathes in the scent common to airport hotels: air freshener and the vaguely rubbery aroma of new carpet. Her heels sink into thick pile that muffles all sound but the low, constant hum of the air conditioning.

When she raps on the door of Room 324, Greg Jackson's voice calls, 'Come in.' He doesn't bother to ask who it is. Who else would be wandering the corridors when everyone else is in bed, asleep or otherwise engaged?

A pass of the master key card lets her inside. She's learned over the years you can tell a lot about a person by the way they treat their hotel room, even if they're only staying for a night. Some keep them almost hygienically neat, as though afraid to upset housekeeping by leaving as much as a damp towel on the bathroom floor. Others litter the room with the contents of their suitcases, sprawling out and treating the place as their own, secure in the knowledge that clearing up after them is someone else's job.

Jackson appears to fall somewhere in the latter camp. A trail of discarded clothes leads from the bed to the bathroom door, the TV is on low, tuned to a 24-hour rolling news station, and the minibar has been raided for its vodka miniatures. Two stand empty, the remaining one waits to be used by the side of a glass in which three or four ice cubes are slowly melting away to nothing.

As for the man himself, he lounges on the edge of the bed, blond hair wet from the shower, a towel wrapped round his waist. His legs are widely spread. Lauren isn't sure whether he intends to give her a flash of his cock, lolling against his thigh and just visible through the opening of the towel. It's certainly big enough that he might enjoy showing it off, out of proportion to his small but muscular frame. But if he was that much of an exhibitionist, she reckons, he'd have opened the door to her in the nude. It wouldn't be the first time that's happened – to Lauren, or to the hotel's constantly changing staff of chambermaids. Some men, it seems, just love to show off everything they've got.

Lauren tries to keep her gaze at eye level, though the flash of Jackson's cock has stirred up a fire in her belly already stoked by thoughts of all the sex that's taken place in the hotel's rooms and her breathless description of Liliana giving Brogan a long, leisurely blowjob.

## Do Not Disturb

There's a stickiness in her panties, her nipples are hard pebbles against the cups of her bra, and she's afraid that she'll have to take a detour on the way back to the front desk, so she can lock herself into a cubicle in the ladies' powder room and bring herself to a swift but oh-so-necessary climax.

She fights to keep her expression neutral as she addresses him, not wanting to give him any clue as to what she can see beneath that towel. 'Your hairdryer, sir.'

Jackson takes it from her, casting a glance at the name badge on her left breast. 'Thanks very much, Lauren.' He grins, revealing slightly crooked white teeth, a little imperfection that only serves to make him more attractive to her eyes. 'There's nothing like being all wet and not able to do a damn thing about it.'

If only you knew, Lauren thinks, feeling another trickle of juice dampening her underwear even further. She never flirts with guests; it's not in her job description. Yet something about this suggestive, handsome Australian makes her want to linger in his room just a little longer. And it's not just the twinkle in his eye or the apparent dimensions of his cock.

'I should take the hairdryer that isn't working,' she tells him. 'The maintenance man will want to have a look at it, see if they can fix it or whether it'll have to be thrown away.'

'Sure thing.' Jackson reaches for the last vodka miniature, twists open the top with an audible crack. He gestures to the socket by the nightstand with the bottle before pouring his drink. 'It's plugged in down there.'

He could very easily unplug the dryer himself, Lauren knows that. But she's sure he wants her to lean over and perform the task so he can take a look at her rear view. The navy blue suit that makes up her receptionist's uniform isn't really designed for women as curvy as her, and the skirt strains taut across her arse as it is. When she bends, the fabric tightens even more, and she's sure the line of her panties will be visible, outlined against the material.

As she tugs the plug free, she hears Jackson's voice close by her ear. 'Oh, very nice,' he purrs. A warm hand stretches out to caress her bum cheeks through the tight-fitting polyester.

He's crossed a line. Looking might be one thing, but touching ... Lauren should leave the room now and scuttle back to the front desk, leaving him to deal with the hard-on that, she discovers when she glances round, is visibly tenting out his towel. But she doesn't. Never mind company policy, with its rigid rules on interaction between staff and guests. Forget that the desk downstairs is unmanned, that her extended absence may be picked up by the closed-circuit TV system designed to add an extra level to hotel security. She wants this handsome, barely clad stranger; wants him with a ferocity that surprises her. And for once, in this bland airport hotel room in the middle of a sultry August night, she's going to make sure she gets what she wants.

Jackson pulls her on to his groin, so his erection butts against her arse. It seems to be seeking out the heat of her sex through her clothing, wanting to bury itself in the cleft between her cheeks. Dropping the broken hairdryer on to the easy chair by the bed, she pushes back at him, blatant in her need. He guides her into position so she's resting on the bed on her elbows, rump in the air. Fingers fumble at the zip of her skirt, and she hears the harsh rasp as he pulls it down. She doesn't resist as Jackson strips her of the unflattering garment, nor when he tugs her regulation tan tights and white cotton knickers all the way down her legs and off.

'Oh, I love a girl with a luscious big arse,' he murmurs, emphasising his point by spreading her cheeks and pushing his nose between them, snuffling at her in his eagerness. Lauren can smell her excitement, a mixture of truffles and brine, and she knows the scent must be stronger where it's concentrated in the dark, hidden crease Jackson begins to explore with long, deft sweeps of his tongue. Desire shudders through her, making her moan and clutch at the satiny burgundy bedcover. She can't see the man's face but she can picture his expression, like a greedy child tucking into his favourite dessert, and the little smacking noises he makes with his lips are an obvious sign of his relish.

This isn't the slow, sensual exploration she's been writing about tonight, the passion of lovers who know each other inside out, and have learned all the tricks that best tease and stimulate. It's something instinctive and primal: two people who will, in all likelihood, never meet again taking advantage of an unexpected opportunity to fuck each other's brains out. The fact that Lauren should be downstairs, keeping an eye on the deserted lobby, instead of sprawling over this bed, half-dressed and with her juices running down her thighs, simply adds extra spice to the occasion.

The point of Jackson's tongue flicks over her clit, before his lips home in on the tender bud, sucking with just the right amount of pressure. Sensation slices through Lauren's body, so strong it almost causes her knees to buckle. This man knows just what he's doing, pushing her with almost indecent haste towards orgasm. When he laps at the entrance to her arse, sliding a finger up into her pussy at the same time, she has to bury her face in the overstuffed pillow and yell out her pleasure, so as not to disturb the guests in the neighbouring room. The windows might be triple-glazed to keep out the noise of aircraft, but the walls aren't quite so thick, and she doesn't want to have her name added to the roster of shame, along with Mr Stocking and the body-paint couple.

When the convulsions of her orgasm finally die away, Jackson spins her round. His towel has come off

## Do Not Disturb

somewhere during the proceedings and his rigid cock pokes up from the trimmed-back hair at his crotch, inviting her to admire it. The smooth, cut length is magnificent, and she stretches out a hand and makes a circle of finger and thumb around it.

Her fist pumps his shaft, back and forth in an unvarying rhythm. Jackson's eyes close and he surrenders to the feel of her fingers. She wanks him to the point where beads of juice glisten at his crown, then holds him steady as her lips plunge in a wet O over the crown and down. Fresh out of the shower, he tastes clean, with just a little hint of lemon verbena soap. Lauren would have preferred him to be riper, the scents of his journey still lingering on him, but, undeterred, she gives herself up to the task of pleasing him the way he's just pleased her. Swirling her tongue round in lazy circles, she lets herself be guided by the hitch in his breathing that tells her he's already tensed himself against coming. Whatever he's doing to prevent himself spilling too soon – thinking about his tax return, worrying whether he'll oversleep and miss his connection in the morning – it seems to be working, as she laves him from root to tip, sucking and tasting every last gorgeous inch of him.

When the pleasure appears to become too much for him, he pulls away, with more than a little reluctance. Lauren sits back on her haunches, watching as he picks up his glass and takes a swig of watery vodka. He offers her some, but she shakes her head. She might have broken so many rules tonight, but she still knows better than to drink on duty.

Somehow, among all the pocket debris on his bedside table, Jackson finds his wallet and the condom lurking within. As he puts it on, Lauren catches sight of herself in the mirror. Above the waist she still looks respectable, even if her hair is coming loose from its neat ponytail, but beneath it she's bare and uninhibited, sex open and shiny-wet from Jackson's oral attention.

He dishevels her appearance even more, tugging open her jacket and blouse so he can free her tits from the cups of her bra. She thinks she sees a jacket button go flying across the room to land under the dresser, where it will no doubt be vacuumed up next time the room is cleaned. Assuming the cleaners bother to vacuum beneath the furniture, that is. It wouldn't surprise her at all if the odd corner is cut from time to time, even in a four-star establishment like this.

Jackson distracts her from her musings by grabbing her legs and pulling her forward, so her arse is positioned right at the edge of the bed. He stands between her parted thighs, smiling down as he enters her with one easy thrust. The thick, condom-clad bar of his cock pushes her walls apart, filling her to a point that's almost, but not quite, too much. Her lips are spread wide, stretched so that her clit is more prominent, more ready to receive stimulation.

## Do Not Disturb

'You like that?' Jackson asks, holding still and letting her get used to the way he feels inside her.

All Lauren can do is nod. She does like it, very much indeed. And if he's even half as good with his cock as he was with his mouth, she knows she's in for the ride of her life.

Sure of her comfort, her consent to what will come next, Jackson thrusts hard, shunting Lauren a little way across the bed. Unsatisfactory thread count or not, the sheets feel good beneath her bare arse, cool and soft.

He grabs her cheeks, partly so he can haul her on to his crotch and partly, she suspects, because he just likes their soft fullness in his hands. Everything that's happened tonight has made it very clear that Greg Jackson is an arse man. Her bare tits bounce indecently with every stroke. It's far from the most dignified fuck she's ever had, but as he bangs into her over and over, she doesn't give a damn. He's so long that the head of his cock is hitting a place inside her most of her lovers have never reached, and the feeling is almost shocking in its intensity.

Lauren moans, lost in bliss, no longer caring if her cries wake whoever's sleeping next door. Let them complain; it's not like there's anyone down on reception to take their call, after all.

He continues to piston into her with measured strokes, steady as the ticking of a grandfather clock. Each one sends powerful shards of feeling through her clit, her belly, her tightly clenched arsehole, winding her whole body in a web of sensation. What Jackson is doing to her is so unbelievably good she wants it to last for ever, but she knows that's not possible. She's racing towards another orgasm, and the way he's humping and grunting, hips moving to a jerky, frantic beat, she knows Jackson's almost there, too.

Another thrust, deeper and harder than before. He's losing his rhythm, his composure, and the veins are standing out like thick cords in his neck.

'Oh, my –' That's the moment when the tension breaks, like water rushing over a dam, carrying her down and down. She drags Jackson with her, the spasms of her vaginal muscles milking his orgasm from him. When it's over he withdraws from her pussy's possessive clasp and slumps, spent and ready for sleep, on the bed beside her.

She untangles herself from his embrace and reaches for her underwear where it lies, tangled up with her tights, on the bedroom floor. 'That was fantastic, but I'd better get back downstairs,' she tells him as she dresses, tucking herself in and making herself look respectable once more. 'There may be other guests who need me.'

Jackson gazes at her with pleasure-glazed eyes. 'I shouldn't really tell you this,' he replies, 'but there was absolutely nothing wrong with the hairdryer.'

'Then why on earth ...?'

He's all too eager to spill his guilty little secret in the

afterglow of good sex. 'I work for the website *Undercover Traveller*. We book into places all round the world and claim to find fault with things, to see how the hotel deals with our complaints, and whether we'd recommend them to people looking for somewhere to stay.'

Lauren should be annoyed at the way he's tricked her, but she can't find it in herself, not after he's fucked her so beautifully. 'Oh, really? And how do you feel you were dealt with on this occasion?'

He grins that slow, sexy grin of his, takes her hand and plants a soft kiss on her palm. 'To my absolute satisfaction, Lauren. To my absolute satisfaction.'

## *Poisons*
## Cèsar Sanchez Zapata

If you let it, masturbation can be a merciless, poisonous death. If you let it get under your skin, it soaks right through to the bone. And how do you know you're dying? Because you feel it, feel it draining the life blood – that's how. That cold, depth-less shrill in your gut when the deed is done. It spreads from your stomach to your chest and you have to suck air in harder just to breathe normally. It makes you conscious of the fact that you're not normal. Because no normal man has to try so hard just to breathe. And then you know your head is infected.

Poisonous bile of momentary pleasure turned to slow death.

You hate yourself. You're dirt. You're old dirt – going on your third decade on this shit-infested planet. She's eighteen. You have no right. You're a dirt shit. She's vibrant and alive. You've already started debating

## Do Not Disturb

whether burial or cremation is the way to go. You've resigned yourself to grey hairs. She's still buying face replenishing lotions to ward off acne. You're a shit that clogs the toilet. A shit that refuses to go down the drain with the rest of the rubbish.

She's your friend's sister.

He's one of those great sort of friends, too. He kept you out of trouble when the trouble seemed to follow you around. He contributed to your survival plenty of times – when even your parents had written you off. Kept you in drinks when you were going through the hardest of times, when he gave up trying to convince you that drinking away wasn't the answer. Everyone has a breaking point. But he's always been there. He was there on the other side of the rabbit hole when you finally climbed out; he never threw it in your face, never said, 'I told you so.' Not once.

You're a piece of corroded shit.

You try and convince yourself it isn't your fault, formulate all manner of justifications. If only the University hadn't flown you into town to deliver a lecture on applied mathematics for the vehicle routing problem. If only she hadn't felt the urge to visit her older brother for the holidays. If only she hadn't heard of you from Terrence, your friend – her big brother. If only big brother hadn't invited you to dinner that night and introduced you right at the table. If only it hadn't been a corner table squeezed in between two others so when you went in for a hug, you had to hold her so tight you were practically inside her. If only she hadn't insisted on wearing such a revealing dress. If only she wasn't so lithe, and firm, and such a breath of fresh air with her perky tits and teasing ass.

If only you hadn't just jerked one off thinking about how sweet she felt against you.

That's where I was.

If only ... but it had felt like that, it really had. She was every inch as supple and limber as that. And she'd pressed her compact little body into me when we embraced. She'd left her mark seared into my chest and smouldering my groin with want. I'd thought of nothing else since. Every nerve and muscle pulsated with desire for her on the cab ride back to the hotel, on the walk through the massive lobby, on the elevator car, in the narrow corridor outside my room. And then, when I could do no more to control the urges, I'd stroked myself with her plundering my mind, whipping my hand up and down like a lunatic, a battering wildebeest, until the cream shot from me in torrents every which way, dousing the entire room in my shame.

The doorbell buzzed and, as if launched from the end of a cannon, like a streak of come I vaulted off the bed. I tugged my pants over my ass and scrambled to the door without checking the peephole. I should have, I know that now. If I had, the whole blundering mess might have been averted. But right then I was still listless and weak-kneed from orgasm, my mind was reeling and my legs felt strangely leaden.

I drew the door open wide, and it was none other than she, the Selena of jism-glutted dreams, that stood firmly at my threshold. She was absolutely magnificent, I couldn't possibly rob her of that; she sported a short denim skirt the only way it was ever meant to be worn – to make slavering idiots of all men. Her tank top, that blessed lamina of gauzy fabric, moulded her tits into something otherworldly.

'Aren't you going to ask me in?' she said. I moved aside. She strolled past me, just like so, and as she did, she ran a playful hand across my crotch, tapping her fingers daintily on my cock. 'What a lovely tent you've erected, Professor. Should I be flattered?'

I stuck my head out and peered down the empty corridor. Then I shut the door. She spun on her heels, her legs spruced straight, boosting her ass exquisitely, and twirling around to me. A move that worked me up something fierce, yet made her seem, if possible, that much younger, and nailed the self-loathing right to my gut. She flipped her hair back over her shoulders, unveiling the deep, sweeping cleavage gushing forth at her neckline.

'How about a drink to wet the throat?' she asked, twining around her fingertip the tiny ringlets of hair behind her ear.

'Out of the question,' I said, perhaps too anxious, because her grin curled higher. She sighed, then, arching her back and stretching the tank top down over the waist of her low-rise skirt, so the hefty bundles promised very definitely to split it in two, rend it like a portière. She stepped directly in front of me, near enough to touch, to run a finger across the sleek, tanned thighs flaunted beneath the hem, close enough to feel and relish. I wanted desperately to taste of her.

'That's not the way to play this, Rico,' she advised. 'It wastes time, can't you see that? We have a limited window of opportunity. Resistance merely postpones the inevitable. And that inevitability is so very much fun. *Believe me.*'

I was caught on her every word, every flicker of her eyelids and twitch in her jaw.

'We'll want as long as we can possibly have to enjoy it.' She hooked her fingers on my fly and tried to pull it down; I swatted her hand away, viciously. She winced at the sting, but damn if that filthy little bitch didn't then crack a smile the likes of which I'd never seen on a woman, lecherous to the point of combustion. She pursed her prurient lips and blew two gusts over the red spot across the back of her knuckles. 'Now *that* we can work with.'

It took every last morsel of verve I had left coursing in my veins, the bit that hadn't been envenomed by lust,

## Do Not Disturb

to turn my back to her, rip the door open and order her to leave. She shook her head, laughing, the rest of her jouncing provocatively.

Take it from me, it is a most daunting and revolting experience to be faced with your own moral weakness, to have it laughed back at you as proof of your succumbing to a war within, to have it skewer you in the guise of a seductress as young as only the devil could make. My spirit was willing to have her out – to kick that bubbly romp square in the middle and send it back whence it came – but the flesh, oh, dear me, the flesh was weak. I had spent my adult life struggling with profound, complex problems, differential equations, variational methods, Newtonian physics. I had conquered them all. But the pull she had on me, this transcendental weight drawing me in at all times, was somehow beyond my understanding. Beyond my strength.

'I really don't understand,' she said, haughtily. 'I thought I made it clear what my intentions were when we met.'

'I suspected.'

'If I'd rubbed my snapper any harder against your leg, you'd have gotten rug burn.'

'I choose to pretend now that I was wrong.'

She shrugged her shoulders, and saying, 'Pretend what you want,' she yanked down on her top harder and that time her tits gave a hearty bounce, and bobbed out. I watched as her nipples furrowed and knitted into tiny studs. She slid one hand down along the robust contours of her body, beyond the skirt, to plunge into her pussy. She jolted straight as an arrow and gasped. Her breathing suddenly became heavy and ragged. I'd never wanted anything as bad as a go at her; the feeling had me wrought, my mind racing, blood pumping. Put mildly, it was overpowering, a straight flux of ardour as potent as a tidal wave. She started rapidly dipping her finger in and out, soaking in the honey that flowed from her, pooled on her sex and ran down the inside of her thighs.

I slammed the door shut again, whipping about in a near sprint. 'Stop that shit,' I scolded. 'Stop it! This isn't a fucking game.'

'That's the first damn thing you've said that made even a speck of sense, Professor. You're right – this isn't a game! I'm randy as hell. If you won't scratch the itch, then I'll do it myself.'

There must have surely been some message that passed between us, some primordial Morse code transmitted by the lids of our eyes, because it rallied us in a minute flat, no less, no more, her staring at me, me staring back, our breaths fusing together, our heat coalescing. I swallowed hard, and she pounced on that piddling sign of weakness with the stealth and agility of a leopard. Then we were trapped in a tornado of flying clothes, swiping hot, frantic touches of one another through the gale of underwear.

## Do Not Disturb

In mere seconds she had my pants open and got a hold of my cock, petting it with her palm vigorously, while the other hand fondled my testicles. 'Without a sense of urgency,' she whispered into the side of my face, all-at-once erudite beyond my expectations, 'desire loses all of its value.'

I flung her onto the bed and turned her onto her hands and knees, her ass jutting straight up. I lunged jaw first, gripping her waist hard, and I ran the tip of my tongue along her snatch up to the tiny, puckering asshole. She had a lovely taste; I'd chew and gorge on it all day if she asked me. From her pussy, the juice seeped like a flood, sluicing over my chin.

'Damn it, I'm *dying* – ram it in already, choke me with it,' she beseeched me, hysterically, one arm clenched between her haunches, opening her snatch wide with sticky fingers. 'Shit, I'm so fucking wet and slimy. Get over here, I want that prick this second or I swear I'll saw it off and skewer myself with it!'

I clambered behind her, scuttled into position, rubbed the head of my cock between her quim's lips. Without further ado, I slipped it in, all of it crammed into her box, then getting right to the dance, the tango, waltz, samba and then some. Her pussy was clutching my root, biting down like it was munching on kielbasa, as we mounted a raving tempo; I battered her, hammering my balls against her ass with every deep thrust through her slippery sex.

I spun her around, hurled her back on the bed and pushed her knees up and apart. Those rosy pink lips pouted open, damp around the cusp of her sex, her clit straining to emerge from between the curtains of flesh. I embedded my face in it, fastening my lips upon the squirmy little nub. She writhed eagerly, heaving and huffing, choking up a storm. She dug her nails into the back of my head so I wouldn't dare to part from her quim; she crushed my nose and mouth to it as she ground her hips into my face. 'Oh, you beautiful fuck. *Oh, fuck!*' Soon after, she stopped moving and I felt her pussy clinched around my tongue, thrumming rabidly.

I crawled atop the wily bitch and pinned her down by the shoulders lest she bludgeon me in her desperate hustle for a good reaming. Quick as a wink, she got a firm grasp of me in her hand and guided me back into her. With a single lunge I buried myself deep inside. She coiled her legs around my waist and lifted herself to meet every thrust. I sucked on her nipples, grazing like some animal out to pasture, nibbling on her teats with my teeth. I pounded my prick in, over and over and over, swollen and nourished by a visceral surge of energy that drove me on, a voltage of raw, unbridled power fuelling me into the blind plunge. In that moment, I felt like a piston, a diesel machine, a mindless mechanism for the furtherance of passion. Her stiletto heels pressed into my back, stabbing the flesh like spurs into a colt.

## Do Not Disturb

I thrust and thrust, raving mad now, screaming, until I swore I heard a snap at the base of my skull. I keeled over the edge, then the only sound left was a low, incessant hum almost like a current sibilating just beneath the surface of my skin.

I withdrew with a sordid pop and collapsed backwards. She scampered up my body, pawing desperately at my legs, slurping my cock into her mouth. No sooner had she wrapped her lips around it than my pecker gave a tiny belch, then erupted to the very back of her gullet. She moaned and closed her eyes, as gouts of jism slid from the corners of her mouth, but she persisted, gobbling up my shaft whole, and drinking the viscous substance. Finally, and truly it seemed like years, my orgasm subsided and she released my prick.

We lay there for a long while, catching our breaths. She stretched out beside me, undulating her hips like a purring feline. Completely satisfied with herself. Her breasts were high and buoyant, breasts such as only youth can sustain: flawless orbs of flesh, years away from drooping, sagging or shrivelling. She ran her nails down the front of my chest. 'Now, wasn't that worth all of those petty guilt trips? Don't they seem pointless?'

I swung my legs off the bed and was sitting on the edge. As I knew it would, the lust to which I'd succumbed evaporated with the drying of my sperm on her chin, and was replaced with a crippling sense of regret. What good is intellect, thought I? What purpose does it serve, if any, and where does it fit in the broad scheme, in the face of such powerful and overwhelming compulsions?

'I wouldn't worry about it much,' she gloated, coolly, as though she were reading my mind. 'It was something you could never hope to resist.'

'We have to tell him,' I said. 'You know we do.'

She propped her legs on the mattress, spreading her knees. She glanced down at her snatch, played a finger on the smooth, moist lips. She tasted herself and me, suckled on the glutinous blend. Then she lit a cigarette, inhaled the smoke deep into her lungs and blew it out in swirling lines that weaved up to the ceiling.

'Tell him, then,' she said. 'It's not me he'll hate. At least, not for the long haul. Me he'll forgive – you'll see. He has no choice, really. Family reunions, Thanksgiving, Christmas ... think about it. He won't be able to ignore me for ever. You, though. You, Professor, he can forget.'

There was logic in those words. I'd known Terrence over twenty years. He was a fair man. He could forget many things, overlook many sins. This, however, banging his little sister, tearing her open like a barnyard animal, Terrence would never forgive. If ever he learned of it –

'I think we still need to tell him.'

'Do what you have to do,' she said. She got off the bed to look at herself in the mirror by the door. She liked her nakedness. I could tell from her expression, the

## Do Not Disturb

way she groomed her hair up over her head and stirred her body in the reflection. I liked it, too, I must confess, and, falling back against the headboard, I feasted my eyes. 'It's funny how men are,' she muttered, mostly to herself, I think. 'How weak they become after fucking.'

I didn't speak.

She turned to me. 'You just spent almost an hour drilling into me like a madman. You pounded me like a beast, you did. I enjoyed it. But look at you now, Professor. Weak. Feeble and spineless. My brother had no place in your mind twenty minutes ago – even your *brilliant* mind. All you wanted was to screw me till one of us was dead. A drop in the bucket – now …'

I reached for the rum bottle on the nightstand. Poured myself a drink, my poison of choice. I lifted the glass to my lips.

'The girl always wins, doesn't she?' she said, in a grandiose manner, as though she'd come finally to an epiphany that had eluded her all her life. That had eluded, perhaps, all the generations that had come before her. 'No matter how much a man gives. No matter how much he thinks he's pleasuring you, maddening you, punishing you … in the end, he's got no power, no control whatsoever. He loses it all the moment he comes.'

I downed the drink in a gulp.

She spun around. Walked to the end of the bed. Peered down at me, at my slumbering prick. She licked her bottom lip, fleetingly, in that way a woman does when she fancies the bits and pieces. I started getting hard again just from the look on her face.

'You're not going to say anything to my brother.'

'I – I have to.'

'No,' she said, slowly, 'you don't.'

She put one knee on the mattress. Then the other. Thus, she hovered above me on all fours.

'He's my best friend. My only friend.'

'And that's why you won't say anything. Good friends are hard to come by.'

'I can't keep it from him.'

'You can.'

Her tits were over my midsection, her rosy nipples pointed down at my shame. My cock was nearly fully erect. It betrayed me. She had me, and she knew it. She bent her head down, smacked her lips. Her eyes stayed unwaveringly on mine.

'You won't say anything.'

Her mouth quivered, then snapped loudly like a Venus Flytrap, *Dionaea muscipula*, inches from the swollen crown of my penis.

'Oh, Jesus. Blow me,' I pleaded. 'Yeah, blow me, please.'

'Will you?'

'Take me in your mouth. Just …' My voice sounded despairing and wretched, even to my own ears. 'Do it now, please. Please!'

## Do Not Disturb

She struck her tongue out like a bullwhip and scourge, the tip of which poised just over my prick. 'You won't say a word.'

'Come on, damn it to hell! Suck me off – suck me off!'

'My brother hears nothing of this.'

I seized her shoulders, and with such savagery hauled her to me, that I could've literally fucked her eye socket. She clamped her lips shut, wrenched her face away.

'Fuck, you little bitch – do it!'

'Say it. I want to hear you say it.'

I shoved her away, disgusted – but not with her. With myself. 'All right! All right, whatever you damn please, I won't tell him a damn thing, *nothing*, just fucking do it already! Just fucking do it – for *fuck's sake*!'

She smiled. She had me. She knew it. I knew it.

'No control,' she said.

Then she lowered her head completely. Her hair flailed over her face and onto my stomach. Her mouth closed over me. It was the damnedest thing. The torment, the curse, the tumult, wickedness and miracles vaporised as soon as she swallowed the length of my cock. Her mouth was like a vacuum of space and time, of sound and sight. The epiphany at that moment was mine. The conclusion was an uncomplicated one. We are all, at all times, dying, hurtling through a sphere of immateriality, of nothingness, so far as we live inhibited. Of one ailment or the other, it does not matter – the deaths are as varied as the diseases. If masturbation is a slow death, then I knew, at that instant, with my prick engulfed in her pretty little mouth, that friendship wasn't a cure. That, you could only take so far. It did only so much to slow the progression into that most indolent demise of monotony – the worst, most tragic of all, for which there had only ever been one cure. A drop of poison to cure all ails.

I reclined my head on the pillow, listening to the soft, wet sucking noises she made.

# Scheduling Conferences
## Kathleen Tudor

Cathy's nerves had been jangling from the moment she'd gotten off the plane, and it seemed like every step made it worse. By the time she'd checked into the hotel, she felt as if her heart was going to burst from her chest, and her fingers and toes actually tingled in anticipation.

She dropped her suitcase onto the hotel-room desk and went straight for the bed. She lay down and closed her eyes, breathing deeply as she tried to calm her racing heart and stop the mild trembling in her limbs. Her entire body seemed to pulse with the force of her anticipation, and she heard the blood pounding in her ears like a chant, *tomorrow, tomorrow, tomorrow.*

With a frustrated cry, she finally gave up on the bed and walked into the bathroom. Crowded and small, it would at least be supplied with the endless hot water that made hotel showers so appealing. She stepped into the hot spray, letting the water sting her skin as she scrubbed sensuously.

Her fingers ran through her wet hair, pulling it gently, and she tipped her head back as she caressed her neck and breasts, letting the simple act of washing become a slow, erotic tease. Her body, already sensitive and flushed with blood, reacted strongly, turning her gentle shaking into a quiver that threatened to rock her off her feet. Her face and breasts became suffused with blood, and her head felt light and dizzy.

She had to sit by the time she got to her pussy, which was drenched and ready. She gasped and threw her head back as her fingers found her hard clit among her folds, and she spread her legs and let the spray of water across her sensitive skin make her whimper and writhe. Images flashed through her mind – his head between her legs, his cock pulsing with eagerness, his eyes fever-bright as he plunged into her – and she felt the orgasm burst over her like a balloon filled with confetti.

She laughed at the image and at the sparkles dancing behind her dizzy eyes, and let herself go limp beneath the hot water, panting and pleasured and yet so far from sated. Her body continued to pulse: *Tomorrow. Tomorrow. Tomorrow.*

It took a sleeping pill to get her to sleep that night, and she woke the next morning feeling tired and uncomfortable from the unnatural rest. She glanced around the room at the unfamiliar surroundings, and it took her a moment to remember where she was and why her heart was beating in a desperate, thready rhythm. Oh, God, *today*!

She considered another shower, but it was getting late, so she reached into her panties and rolled over onto her belly, grinding against her hand to work out some of the morning's nervous energy. Her breath came in short pants and gasps, and she whimpered as she felt the pleasure build inside her. *Yes! God!* 'Erik! Fuck!' It was less dramatic this time, simply flowing through her like a wave, taking away some of the nerves and bringing a sense of calm and wellbeing. For the moment.

Cathy dressed smartly and took the time to style her hair and apply her make-up with care. She cursed when she saw the time, and hurried downstairs. She registered at the desk that had been set up in front of the ballrooms, giving her name to the unsmiling woman – who had probably only volunteered to get a discount on her admission – then took her nametag and her programme and wandered into the conference.

She grabbed a bagel from one of the tables placed within the conference perimeter, glad that the organisers had planned for feeding the hordes of attendees who were too rushed or excited or scattered to have planned their meals better. Another glance at the time sent her scrambling through her programme. There! Her first opportunity would be in one hour.

With her fingers shaking slightly less, and her body settling from over-stimulation to a mere buzz of impatience, she scanned the programme again, selected a workshop that she was only slightly late for and found the hall quickly.

The class was interesting, and she sat near the back, taking notes in the notebook she always kept in her purse, but otherwise remaining quiet and unobtrusive. She was one of the first out the door when the workshop concluded, and made her way straight to the room where Erik would be presenting. Though it was a large hall, she felt drawn to the correct room, as if her body was responding to Erik's very presence.

She found a seat near the middle, pulled out her Kindle and scanned the words of a story without absorbing them, trying to keep her mind busy. Her heart stuttered when he walked into the room, and she followed his progress without lifting her head. First, he set up his notes, then he got a bottle of water from a table in the corner. He paced the front of the room, and she blushed every time his eyes flitted to her. *Yes, I'm here. I'm ready. Oh, God!*

The seats around her slowly filled, and she finally put the Kindle away, giving up on the pretence of reading. She glanced at the programme again, to plan. He was doing a presentation on how to increase your productivity without sacrificing quality, and giving examples of the kinds of mistakes editors often catch when writers are hurrying. Well, that would make it easy, then!

*Do Not Disturb*

She fidgeted and squirmed until the presentation began, and then watched avidly, taking in every nuance of Erik's voice without actively hearing much of what he was saying; she'd heard it all before from him, anyway, and the presentation wasn't why she was here.

When he finally opened up the floor for questions, she had to exercise strict control to keep her hand from shooting straight up. He called on two people before her, and she sat patiently, knowing it would only be a matter of time.

'Thank you,' she said when he gestured to her. 'I keep track of my writing time, and I average a pretty clean manuscript at 1322 words per hour. Do you have any particular tricks for picking up my speed?'

Erik smiled. 'That's a good question. When you've already got a very good pace, sometimes it comes down to planning. For example, knowing what you're going to write, at least in a general sense, before you sit down to write it. You can also definitely try tracking what time you write best. For example, if you get the most efficient work done at 3 p.m., then definitely try to schedule your work around that time.'

She murmured a quiet thanks. *Three o'clock.*

He dismissed the workshop at noon exactly, and she made her way to the luncheon, where a keynote speaker was giving a droning talk that was probably meant to be inspirational. She picked at a soggy fruit salad and an onion roll sandwich as she browsed the programme. Might as well choose a couple more workshops and make the best of her time.

But, halfway through the next workshop, she was too impatient to sit still a moment longer. She waited for a lull in the speaker's presentation, then edged out with an apologetic smile to the woman at the front of the room, and made her way up to her room – room 1322.

There wasn't much she could do to prepare, but she did what she could think of, putting her clothes away and stashing her suitcase in the closet, then changing out of the flattering suit and into an even more flattering set of purple and black lingerie. She twirled in front of the full-length mirror on the closet door, struck a pose and examined herself from every angle. She restyled her hair, frowned, brushed it out and then spritzed it with water and let her natural curls take over. She washed her face, studied every line and pore and, with a sigh, reapplied the make-up.

She was lying on the bed, considering pleasuring herself again, when she heard a quiet tap at the door, and her heart pounded as if it wanted to escape her chest. A glance at the clock on the bed table showed that it was 3.05, and, for the first time that day, she thanked God that time was finally on her side.

Erik stood on the other side of the door, looking dark and roguish. He dressed like a professor, but his tie was already loosened and his hair was mussed as if he had been running his hands through it. She almost expected to see ink stains on his palms, but with modern technology such things were nonsense. It was too bad; he would have looked sexy with inky fingers.

Of course, he already looked sexy. She grabbed him by the loosened tie and pulled him into the room, and he came into her arms in a heartbeat, his tongue already sliding into her mouth before she even heard the door click shut. They stumbled towards the bed, neither willing to let the other go long enough to undress properly, and a scattering of shoes and pieces of his clothing trailed them all the way to the bed.

Beside the mattress, she pulled his cock free, and their kiss broke as she dropped to her knees in front of him. She took a moment to appreciate the sight of his cock and breathe in the deep, musky smell of him before she sucked the tip into her mouth and swirled her tongue all around his crown, making him moan.

His fingers burrowed into her hair and tangled, pulling as he encouraged her to feast. 'Cathy, you gorgeous, sexy bitch. Oh, shit, you were always so fucking good at that. Oh, *God* ...' He trailed off into a moan as she sucked him deep into her throat, burrowing her nose into his dark curls for a moment, holding it as long as she could, and swallowing around him until her throat ached.

When her lungs burned for air, she eased back and

started to feast in earnest. 'Oh, baby, I can't believe I wait months for this. You're *killing* me! I had to jerk off twice yesterday just to contain myself. Wow, just like that. Oh, yeah, baby.' She purred at his words. It *had* been a long few months, and it got harder and harder to wait, the longer this little affair went on. Not that either of them was in a relationship, but that didn't make their meetings any less forbidden.

But God, wasn't it the naughtiness of it all that made it so hot? Attending the same conferences, finding ways to pass their room numbers and meeting times, and holy *shit* was her pussy wet from the anticipation. She reached into her lace panties and moaned as she found the moisture pooled there, soaking through the scrap of fabric that covered her and dampening patches of her thighs.

Erik's voice broke as he continued to praise her skills, and he moaned, his ass twitching in what she had come to recognise as the telltale sign that he was about to come. She sucked his cock deep into her throat and felt it pulse and throb as he groaned and shot his load, and she paused there, milking him dry with her swallows as he pulled at her hair and ground into her.

When he was reduced to ragged breathing, she eased back and smiled up at him from her place on the floor, knowing how it must look to see her down there beside his spent cock like a little vixen.

He groaned and pulled her to her feet, and they came together again in a kiss that made her toes curl and her entire body tingle with wave after wave of goosebumps. Erik pushed her onto the bed and stood for a moment admiring her before he took hold of the tiny scrap of lace posing as panties and drew it down her legs. He took a deep breath and grinned, and she knew that it must be suffused with her scent, wet as it was.

'I want your tongue in my hole,' she said. He moaned and moved for her, his face going immediately for her pussy as she spread her legs wide for him. She cried out when his tongue teased over her slit, and then nearly growled with frustration as he took the time to suck her labia teasingly into his mouth, first one, then the other.

She reached between her legs to tug on a lock of his hair, and he chuckled into her pussy and delved deeply into her molten centre, fucking her hard with his tongue and pausing from time to time to lap at the rest of her pussy, vocalising his enjoyment of her taste in moans and hums and growls of pleasure.

Cathy made plenty of noise of her own, gasping and moaning approval of his technique. 'I can't believe it's been three months. *Fuck*, I've missed this. Oh, holy shit, Erik, that's so good, fuck me deep.' She bucked her hips towards his face, savouring the sensation, and cried out when he reached up from between her legs to clamp his fingers around one of her nipples, to tug and tease it as he fucked her with his tongue.

His breath was hot and heavy between her legs, making Cathy whimper with anticipation. Every nerve in her body was lit up like Christmas, sending her into a warm, glowing space that got hotter every second. 'I love this so much. Suck my clit. Make me come!' Her vision seemed to crack and shatter when he obeyed, and as his mouth clamped around her clit, her legs followed suit, squeezing his head as her whole body rocked with pleasure.

Her vision went white and a rushing sound filled her ears, then slowly filtered back to reveal that she was issuing a high-pitched whine of ecstasy. She stopped when she realised, and unclamped her knees from around Erik's head. He sat up grinning, and she propped herself up on her elbows, legs splayed, to eye him back.

'Hey,' she said, still a little breathless.

'Hey, yourself.' He didn't sound so steady, either, and it made her grin.

'How have you been?'

'Oh, the usual. Can't tell you how much I missed this, though. I think you look even hotter than last time.' His cock stirred as if to underline the words, and he grinned roguishly.

'I've been working out,' she said. Her words and tone remained casual, but her body was still heavy with desire, and sitting with her pussy on display to him was keeping her flushed with arousal.

## Do Not Disturb

'How much time do you have?' he asked, moving up the bed towards her. His cock stirred again, and she reached out to stroke a single finger down its length, making it jump.

'I'm on that stupid author panel at 7,' she said, shrugging. 'It will take me less than ten minutes to get dressed and get down there if I'm motivated.'

He grinned and kissed her, his tongue teasing over her lips before slipping into her mouth, then back to brush lightly over her lips again, soft then deep, making her tremble. He pulled back a moment later, or an hour, she had no idea. 'I'll have to see to it that you're motivated, then.'

His inkless fingers wrapped around his cock, and he stroked slowly, letting her watch. Her eyes followed the movements as it grew thicker and longer beneath his hand, and each time it pulsed and swelled, her breath grew faster and harder until she was staring at his cock like a starving woman at a feast, panting with desire.

'Turn over,' he said, and she hastened to obey. He grabbed her hips and pulled her towards him, positioning her with her ass in the air, on display. 'Gorgeous,' he breathed, and the tip of his cock butted up against her wet hole. She whimpered, and he laughed and teased her, sliding his cock across her wetness without delving within.

'Damn it, Erik, fuck me,' she moaned, and with another laugh he complied. His cock slid into her like it belonged, and she pushed back, driving him deep as her pussy stretched to accommodate him. It had been too long. Too fucking long!

'Do you want it rough?' he asked. His voice was ragged as he controlled his slow strokes.

'Yes. Fuck me hard. Oh!' He slammed into her, making her gasp, and his hand immediately tangled in her hair, pulling it and forcing her to arch back and press even harder into him. 'Yes! Oh, shit, yes! Fuck me. Fuck me!' No one else had ever inspired her to talk like this, but with him it had always been natural. Everything about their covert relationship screamed of naughtiness and smut, and nothing in her life had ever been so titillating or felt so right.

His cock rammed into her again and again, and he grunted with each thrust, burying himself deep inside her. And with each thrust, each grunt, her responding moan rose higher and higher in pitch until she was singing breathily, her entire body strung as tight as a wire as she cried out.

She reached between her legs and found her clit, engorged and desperate for touch. Each brush of her fingers became an exquisite torture, sometimes soft, sometimes harder as he slammed into her and threatened her control. Her neck ached from being pulled back, and somehow the discomfort only channelled further into her pleasure as he took her, rough and wild like they were a pair of animals.

## Do Not Disturb

'OhGodohGodyesyes!' She shook so hard that she lost contact with her clit, but it didn't matter – nothing could stop the tidal force of her orgasm once it had started, and the incredible sensation of him pounding into her only heightened her pleasure. She felt herself contract hard around him, and Erik started to lose his rhythm as his body took control, finding his own release.

She let her upper body collapse onto the bed as his grip on her hair loosened and he roared with pleasure and drove himself into her a couple more times. Then he let himself collapse beside her, and they both lay panting for several long moments.

'You're going to wear me out,' he teased.

'We'll go slower next time.' She shifted until she lay within the circle of his arms, and their legs tangled together as they kissed, slow and sensual. He was her editor at Riverstone Press, and forbidden by company policy to have an outside relationship with any of his authors, but the first time they'd met at a conference, sparks had flown before they'd exchanged names and made the unfortunate connection. The man who polished her books to perfection was also the forbidden man who made her heart stutter and her knees weak. And, as they'd discovered later, could drive her to some of the most powerful orgasms of her life.

Or make her melt into a puddle of warm pleasure, as he was doing now. Between the soft sweetness of his kisses and the way his hands brushed gently over every inch of skin he could reach, her body was humming with sensual energy – something more toned down than the erotic explosions before, but just as powerful. She sighed into his mouth, and felt him swallow up her pleasure and feed it back to her through his fingertips.

His touches went from featherlight to something more teasing, and he used his nails, scraping them across her skin in swirls and patterns that made her gasp and shiver and moan helplessly beneath his touch. His cock stirred against her belly, but neither of them made any move towards it this time, merely adjusting to accommodate the increasing presence as she continued to lie passively aroused by his manipulations.

When his hands both rose to splay over her breasts, Cathy tossed her head back and broke the kiss, a soft mew escaping her as he cupped and weighed them in his strong hands. His fingers teased around her nipples until she pressed forwards, using her body to beg for more. He gave it, pinching and twisting her nipples gently until she was nearly crying with the pressure of desire.

Then he swept her close with one arm and let the other drift even farther down her body until he cupped her pussy with his hand. 'Do you want to come?' he whispered into her ear.

She shivered. 'Please ...'

His fingers slid inside her and he pressed the heel of

his hand against her clit, rocking his palm in the perfect pattern to set her on fire. He had lost nothing of his technique in the months since they'd last lain this way.

She kissed him again, and tried to focus on the soft texture of his mouth against hers, delaying the orgasm that rose inevitably before her, feeling the magnitude of it increase with every second she put it off. Finally, it overwhelmed her ability to distract herself, and she cried out into their kiss as her body shook with the force of it. He held his fingers still within her until she'd calmed, then slid them free and licked her juices from them.

She moaned as she watched him, and he grinned. He pressed on her shoulder, rolled her flat on her back and slid into her with one quick motion. Her pussy, still tingling in the after-effects of the last orgasm, seemed to burst to life, and she cried out again and clung to him as he rocked softly against her.

'That's my beautiful girl,' he whispered. 'God, you feel so amazing. It's been for ever. Oh, *God*, this is perfect.'

He took his time, teasing her with long, slow strokes, bringing her to the brink of orgasm again and again before pulling back or changing rhythm or simply freezing within her until Cathy was incoherent with pleasure and desire and the desperate, animal urge to come. And when he finally couldn't take any more, he thrust into her at just the right angle, stroking her clit with his pubic bone as he fucked her, until they came together, both trembling and exhausted.

It was long moments before Cathy felt capable of speaking. 'Do I have time to shower?'

'It's almost six.' She glanced at him, and he gave her a wicked grin. 'I don't think I could get it up again before your panel if my life depended on it, but that doesn't mean I can't torture you while you wash.'

She laughed and climbed shakily to her feet. 'I have a second room key on top of the television. You can move your stuff in while I'm presenting. And order some food, will you? I'm going to be dying by the time we finish.'

'I already miss you,' he teased, though there were two more days of the conference. 'When's the next one?'

'We're already signed up for the big one in Denver in two months, but there's a tiny conference in some little town in Michigan in three weeks. They emailed me about filling in for a presenter who cancelled.'

'Bet I could get in on that. They always get excited when editors volunteer for the pitch sessions,' he said, grinning.

She kissed him and preceded him to the shower, where he reminded her how much fun she could still have with a flaccid cock. Thank goodness for the unlimited hot water.

She was ten minutes late for her own panel, but, since she had developed a reputation at conferences for being a little scattered, no one gave it a second thought.

## *Ssshh No Speaking!*
### Tabitha Kitten

I lock my car, take a deep breath and walk over to the hotel. After weeks of emails, texts and telephone conversations Richard and I have decided to meet up and role-play our combined sexual fantasy.

It's astonishing to consider that only three months ago I had never heard of Richard, but now I am about to spend the night with him, will have sex with him – a man whom I have never met. And that is what makes this encounter so thrilling.

I had come into contact with Richard on a dating website. He had described himself and sent me several photographs; most of them were of his physique, which was impressive. And although his eyes were obscured by his shades, on a full picture of his body in profile I had liked what I had seen. Flirty emails and texts ensued and several telephone conversations where we talked into the small hours about everything and nothing. As time progressed our emails became raunchier and steamier. Finally, we'd decided that we wanted to meet up. Originally, we had planned a dinner date but we both knew that the restaurant meal was just a prelude to going to bed. And, with this thought nestling in the backs of our minds, we had spoken about what we would like, our first time in the bedroom. On the telephone Richard had admitted, 'Lisa, I have this fantasy, this sexual fantasy.'

'Mmm, I'm listening,' I had replied cautiously.

'I'm sitting in a hotel bar, and this woman walks in, a complete stranger. We don't speak to each other but we leave the bar together. We go to a room, have fantastic sex all night long, in different positions – we have oral, we have anal, but we never once speak to each other. And in the morning we just get up, dress and leave, never having spoken.'

I laughed. 'Well, I suppose we are strangers in one respect because we haven't actually met each other before.'

Hesitantly he asked, 'Would you be up for it?'

It would be an incredible way to start our relationship. I didn't need to think about it for long. 'Yes, Richard, I would.'

'Oh, that's brilliant.' There was relief in his voice. 'And what about you? Is there anything you would particularly like whilst we are together?'

## Do Not Disturb

I paused. 'Actually, I adore being tied up. I'd love it if you would tie my hands to the bed, straddle me so I can give you head and then, when you're ready, just hold my legs up high and fuck me.'

Richard's breathing sounded heavier. I think he was getting aroused at our plans for our first meeting.

'Yes, I could do that.'

'But Richard, your fantasy, the anal sex part – I've never had anal sex before.' I paused. 'It'll be my first time but, yes, I am prepared to try it.'

Richard must have become more inflamed, because when he replied his words sounded garbled. 'Yes, I'll be very careful.'

'So we'll forget about having dinner beforehand. I'll just meet you in a hotel bar and we'll see how it goes.'

'No speaking, though,' he reminded me.

'No speaking,' I confirmed.

\* \* \*

I walk purposefully through Reception, deliberately avoiding eye contact with the hotel staff, and head for the bar. I have been preparing myself for this encounter for several days. I am wearing a cobalt-blue shift dress, black stockings and black stilettos. Beneath my dress I wear a red and black basque because Richard had confided earlier that he found them very erotic. He had also mentioned, laughingly, that he found a shaven pussy exciting, so I am now totally hairless and without panties. I want this fantasy to be played out so well. Earlier, this morning, I had gone to a local haberdashery store and purchased four long lengths of silk material to use as restraints. My bag is full of items bought especially for tonight.

My heart is racing as I push the door open and walk into the bar. Instrumental music plays quietly in the background. There is a middle-aged couple sitting nearby and, on the far side, two men discuss the documents laid out on the table in front of them. And, sitting at the bar, with his back to me, is Richard. Casually, I stroll over. He glances up at me as I stand alongside him. We had agreed previously that if we didn't fancy each other when we met up either of us could leave, no questions asked.

'A gin and tonic, please,' I order when the barman approaches. I sit on the stool next to Richard. He has his mobile phone on the counter and is tapping away at the keys.

Trying to appear nonchalant I turn to look at him as I wait for my drink. He has thick, dark hair that curls rather boyishly at the nape of his neck. There is a faint trace of stubble on his jaw and his eyes are a deep green and glint invitingly in the sombre room. He has broad shoulders and well-manicured hands. He looks marginally older than I had imagined him but in the flesh he is incredibly handsome.

## Do Not Disturb

I pay for my drink. I'm very nervous but Richard and I have written and talked about this evening many times. It's our fantasy that we're about to enact. I edge towards him and nudge the back of his leg with my foot. A brief look of surprise flashes across his face but he continues to drink. I massage his leg with my foot and then lean forwards, resting my hand lightly on his thigh. Whilst holding my glass with my left hand I tenderly squeeze and rub his thigh with my right. He turns to face me and I smile widely; he smiles back and I feel reassured. He's about to speak so I put a finger swiftly to his lips.

'Ssshh, you know the rules, no speaking.'

I continue to caress his thigh, ensuring that my hand accidentally brushes his groin. The thought of the naughtiness that awaits me makes me tingle and I'm impatient to leave the bar. I finish my drink quickly and then nod towards the lift. Richard rises to his feet and I follow him out of the bar. I'm so excited I can already sense my pussy pulsating.

Inside the lift the sexual tension is palpable. Teasingly, I hitch up my dress so that Richard can see my stocking-tops, and then slightly higher so that he can see my hairless pussy, now slick with my juices. The lust is apparent in his dark-green eyes. He lunges at me and grabs my bottom, pulling me against him so that I can feel his erection.

I follow him along the corridor to his room. There is

a four-poster bed and on either side is a standard lamp that bathes the room in a subdued light. The heavy curtains are closed and beneath them are a Victorian desk and two large leather chairs. There is a wardrobe and opposite is the en-suite. I open my bag and, on the desk, lay out the items for tonight: a box of condoms; a blindfold; the four silk scarves; a vibrator and a bottle of anal lubricant.

Standing behind me Richard unzips my dress and I wriggle out of it. He scoops my hair from my neck and kisses the bare skin. I tremble at the sensitivity of his lips and the warmth of his breath. His hands slide around my waist, up my body to my breasts, finding their way into the fine material of the cups of my basque. Playfully, he rolls my erect nipples between his thumbs and forefingers. Desire sears through me. He continues to kiss my neck and tease my nipples and, hungrily, I reach behind, searching for his groin. I feel his erection beneath the material of his trousers and rub seductively. In response he bites my neck hard and pinches my nipples. I'm overwhelmed by passion.

Richard moves to the desk and picks up one of the silk scarves. He places my wrists together in front of my body and wraps the scarf around them and tics it. He then takes the blindfold and slips it over my eyes. Instantly, I feel vulnerable and highly aroused. He pushes one of his fingers into my mouth. Now that I have no vision, my other senses come to the fore; I pick up the sound of his breathing, the smell of his aftershave, the taste of his skin and the feel of his finger upon my tongue. I suck it and imagine that it is his cock.

He stops and bends me over. I realise he is sitting on the edge of the bed and he pulls me down so that I'm across his lap. He yanks the scarf taut so that my arms are against his calf and then traps the end of the material beneath his feet. He starts to caress my buttocks, kneading the flesh and digging his fingers roughly into the skin. Silently, I'm willing him to touch my pussy; it's aching to feel his fingers. As if knowing my thoughts, Richard moves from my buttocks to between my legs. He runs a finger along my pussy and I moan with sweet satisfaction.

'Naughty girl,' I hear him murmur.

And then he smacks my arse. The suddenness of it makes me writhe but he puts his left arm firmly across my back to hold me in place on his lap. Then he starts up a rhythm: stroke my gaping pussy to make me moan; spank my right buttock hard; stroke my gaping pussy to make me moan; spank my left buttock hard, like he's punishing me for enjoying it. Each time he spanks me he moves to a different place so that soon all the skin is tingling and smarting. I'm so turned on that I'm wet.

He starts massaging my tender skin with strong but soothing strokes, and then releases the scarf and sits me on the bed. I can hear him walking around the room and the sound of the chairs being moved. My bottom stings but, mainly, I'm aware of the lascivious ache deep within my pussy. I need his fingers and cock inside me.

His arms around me, he gently tugs to indicate he wants me to get on the floor. This surprises me – why does he want me on the floor when there is a beautiful four-poster bed here? He has placed two pillows on top of each other and he makes me kneel on them. Pulling the scarf, he forces me down and forwards, and places my hands so that I'm gripping the desk leg. The silk material swishes softly across my arms and behind my neck. He's tied me firmly so that my face is almost touching the carpet and I can't raise my head. He spreads my knees and I know that my pussy is exposed and available to him. I feel a scarf being tied around my left thigh and the other end around my left ankle, but he must have threaded the material around the chair arm, because there is a strain on the scarf and I can't move my leg. He does the same to my right leg, binding me somehow to the chair. I can't close my thighs; I'm bound securely to the hotel-room furniture, my head held low and my arse sticking majestically in the air. Being tied up like this, offering my pussy to him, makes me feel very wanton and sexy. I imagine him standing there, admiring the way I am whorishly on display, looking at my sex glistening with the juices from my desire.

## Do Not Disturb

The noises I can hear tell me Richard is undressing, getting a condom from the box and putting it on. I'm almost shaking from anticipation, not knowing if, when he touches me, it will be with his tongue, his fingers or his cock. He's kneeling behind me. And, suddenly, it happens. He just plunges his finger inside me and starts to finger-fuck me, fast and furious. Bound, there is nothing I can do but accept this pussy-pummelling. I'm panting loudly and aware of the wet sound of his finger sliding in and out of my sodden sex. He starts to rub my clit and I bite my lip to try and suppress my shrieks of delight. And then he stops, and begins to smack my shaven pussy. No man has ever done this before and I've obviously been missing out. Arousal surges through me. The frantic fingering recommences, and, although he's only been touching me for a couple of minutes, I think I'm going to come. When he clasps my clit again I'm convinced of it. Before I realise it I'm begging, 'Fuck me. Please. Fuck me now, Richard.'

'What did you just say?' he asks surprised.

I grimace. I know we're not meant to talk but that slipped out inadvertently. He stops playing with me and my body relaxes as the imminent orgasm subsides. I breathe deeply as I come down and try to control myself. After a few seconds he starts another onslaught, fingering me again with force, and immediately I'm back there at the brink. I wrestle with my restraints, not wanting to come until he's inside me. Desperately I scream, 'Just fuck me now, Richard, fuck me hard.'

He grabs my hips and slams his cock full into me. I cry out as my yielding pussy takes it all. He pumps lustily whilst again kneading my buttocks and grasping handfuls of my flesh. I'm glad I have the desk leg to grip because I'm using it to push myself back on to his cock, feeling his full length rammed inside me. He does indeed fuck me hard, showing my pussy no mercy as he thrusts deep, making me writhe on his thick, powerful cock. I have so wanted this, my dream of bondage with Richard in a hotel room. Blindfolded, bound and fucked. He reaches between my legs and starts rubbing my clit vigorously, and within seconds I'm bucking and jerking as I shatter through my crashing climax. My muscles tighten and I can feel him shuddering as he comes. It was fast but it was one helluva fuck.

He stands up and I wait for him to free me from my silken restraints but instead he goes into the bathroom. I hear the shower being switched on. Alone, tied up and in my own world of darkness, he leaves me on the floor for what seems like ages. My legs and back are beginning to ache. I want to stretch. Finally, I hear the bathroom door open and he returns. He kneels behind me.

'Are you OK?' he asks quietly.

'Yes.'

'Good, because I'm about to fuck you again.'

## Do Not Disturb

I quiver at his words and, when I hear the sound of him removing another condom from the box, excitement swells within me. I wait for the touch of his hand on my insatiable pussy but it doesn't happen. Instead I gasp loudly and shiver as cold dollops of lubricant drop into the crack of my arse. It's going to happen! This is what I have been fantasising about since Richard first mentioned it: my virgin bottom being violated by his magnificent cock. I breathe in deeply at the feeling of him prising my buttocks apart and rubbing the lubricant along my butt crack. And when he applies mild pressure to my puckered hole, I squirm with expectancy. Over and over, he presses down on my tightness, knowing I'm getting more and more excited. Finally, he penetrates me, forcing me open with his finger. Involuntarily, I squeeze as my muscles feel this intrusion. My breathing is shallow and quick and I'm engulfed with longing, ashamed to realise I'm rocking back and forth to lift my arse up to him, helping him to slide his finger in and out. With slow and measured jabs he finger-fucks my arse. And it is wonderful. As he pushes in another finger I whimper at the delectable way I'm being stretched.

'Oh, Richard,' I pant.

'Why do you keep calling me Richard?' he asks.

Abruptly, I stop rocking and stiffen. 'What do you mean? You're Richard,' I say sharply.

'No. My name's Andy.'

'Don't mess around, Richard,' I snap.

He reaches forward and the movement causes his fingers to shove further inside me and I gasp. The blindfold is lifted up. I blink painfully in the sudden light but, when I focus, I see in front of me, on the carpet, a company's ID badge. The photograph is clearly of the man who has two fingers up my arse. Andrew Ballinger.

I go cold with the awful realisation. I have just been fucked by a complete stranger! Oh, God!

'I thought you were Richard,' I mumble. 'I'm meant to be with Richard.'

Andy replaces the blindfold and I descend into darkness again. I'm panicky; I'm bound by a man I know nothing about and he has his fingers embedded in my arse.

'I have to go,' I mutter.

He ignores me and asks instead, 'What's your name?'

'Lisa,' I say quietly.

He clamps his free arm around me, holds me tight against his body and restarts his finger-fucking of my backside, picking up speed, a much faster rhythm now, one that makes me cry out loudly and causes my pussy to ache.

Oh, hell, this feels amazing. But it's not Richard. 'No, no, you shouldn't be doing that,' I cry.

'Why not? You're loving it.' He pushes harder and, unintentionally, I moan with pleasure.

'But you're not Richard,' I manage to blurt out.

## Do Not Disturb

'So, Lisa, tell me about Richard. How come you didn't realise I wasn't him?'

I can hardly speak. My muscles are tight and I'm panting so heavily from his relentless fingering of my arse that my words are rushed. 'I met him on the internet but we haven't actually met yet. We were going to meet for the first time tonight in the bar downstairs. We were going to role-play two strangers meeting in a bar, going to a hotel room, no speaking allowed, and then fucking all night long.'

Andy laughs. 'Including bondage and anal sex. God, that is so horny. So very horny.' He keeps on fingering me.

'You need to stop,' I whine. 'I have to go.'

'But you're loving it. Admit it.'

Andy removes his fingers and releases his grip on me. I must go and find Richard. But his hands are again on my bottom and once more he gently parts my buttocks. His cock is pressing against my anus. This man is not Richard but, oh, God, I so want this. I'm pushing against him. He holds my hips to steady himself. And, in the way he teased me with his fingers he does the same with his cock. Just a moderate pressure and then away, tormenting me, making me think he is about to enter me but then stopping.

'Well, Lisa, it's your choice,' he says. 'I can either untie you and you can get dressed, collect your playthings and see if your Richard is still in the bar waiting or ...' He pushes the tip of his cock into my arse. I have never heard myself pant or moan this loudly before. His cock is edging me open. 'Or I can continue to fuck you and you can stay here with me tonight.'

Just the tip is inside, entering me, then a little bit more. He moves in and out ever so slightly, almost imperceptibly, but it sends shockwaves through me.

'Shall I continue?' he asks.

'God, yes, yes, Andy. Please don't stop.' I can't believe how throaty and guttural my voice sounds.

Slowly, so slowly, he pushes himself in further. My muscles expand reluctantly to take the girth of his thick cock, trying to contract and push him back out. He holds himself in this position, feeling my muscles tight around the tip of his cock. It hurts accommodating his swollen member, the way he strains my muscles, but I know my greedy arse is opening up for him, allowing him entry. With the lightest of movements he inches in and out and I'm screaming in ecstasy. I grip the desk leg tightly as he fucks me so slowly and gently. The sensation is unbelievable; I feel the pleasure rising in my arse in the same way that it does in my pussy when I'm about to come. It keeps increasing and increasing. No, it is becoming unbearable. I need to come. Oh, hell, how I need to come. I clench my pussy muscles to try and bring myself off but that doesn't work. My thighs are still held apart by the scarves. I can't rub my legs together to gain relief. This is too much, I can't take any more. This man is killing me, I need him to touch my sex. Urgently.

I yell, 'God, I need to come. Make me come'

'Soon,' he whispers.

'No. Now. Please, please,' I beg.

He smacks my arse. 'When I'm ready.' He fucks me some more; hardly moving his cock but enough to drive me wild. Then, at last, he massages my clit and the feel of his touch is the catalyst for my climax. Immediately I thrash, uncontrolled, and it pushes me further on to him. With each jolt I'm forcing him deeper into me; impaling myself on his prick. He pounds into me and I feel so gloriously, satisfyingly full – full of cock, so full of cock. Being fucked in the arse is everything I ever imagined it would be. I come, violently and noisily. It is the most intense orgasm I have ever experienced. There is a rush in my head and I'm not sure if it's the effect of wearing the blindfold or whether, for a second, I do black out. Breathless, I collapse on to the carpet.

Andy spanks me hard several times before withdrawing but I'm too exhausted to care. He unties the scarves and then goes into the bathroom. I'm so stiff; unable to stand, I roll on to my side and remove the blindfold. Listening to the sound of Andy's shower, I lie on the floor appalled at what I've just done. Eventually, I stand and retrieve my phone. I had switched it to silent mode; I have six texts, three missed calls and one voicemail from Richard.

*Hi, Lisa. I got stuck in traffic and was thirty minutes late. I can't see you anywhere in the bar. Have you arrived yet? I'm going to wait in the bar until about ten. Let me know what's happening. I'm really looking forward to tonight. Richard.*

Andy walks out of the bathroom, a towel wrapped around his waist. He smiles broadly as he sits down on the bed. Embarrassed, I rush to the bathroom. In the mirror I see my bottom still pink from the spanking, my swollen pussy, open and used, and my freshly fucked arse. Hastily I freshen up.

Richard will still be downstairs. I can get dressed and leave here and be with him in five minutes. I could be with the man whose fantasy I'm meant to be sharing. I peek around the bathroom door. Andy has tied a scarf to each corner of the bed. The blindfold, vibrator and a condom are on the pillow. I step back before he sees me. Once he has bound me spread-eagled to the bed, he intends to blindfold me, use the vibrator on me and then fuck me. My pussy throbs at the thought.

I bring up Richard's contact details on my phone and send a text.

*Dreadfully sorry, Richard, but my car has broken down. I'm not going to be able to get there tonight. Really sorry it's taken me so long to let you know what's happened. Can we reschedule please to another night? I will certainly make it up to you.*

## *Do Not Disturb*

Switching off my phone I re-enter the bedroom.

Andy is holding the end of one of the scarves ready to bind me. 'No speaking,' he says.

I agree. 'No speaking. Just fucking.'

www.ingramcontent.com/pod-product-compliance
Ingram Content Group UK Ltd.
Pitfield, Milton Keynes, MK11 3LW, UK
UKHW041209180426
11947UKWH00025B/1949